SPIES' WIVES

SPIES' WIVES

STORIES OF CIA FAMILIES ABROAD

KAREN L. CHIAO
AND
MARIELLEN B. O'BRIEN

CREATIVE ARTS BOOK COMPANY
Berkeley · California

Cover designed by Barbara A. Stitt

SPIES' WIVES is published by Donald S. Ellis
and distributed by Creative Arts Book Company

For information contact:
Creative Arts Book Company
833 Bancroft Way
Berkeley, California 94710
1-800-848-7789

ISBN 0-88739-321-7
Library of Congress Catalog Number 99-68402

Printed in the United States of America

A NOTE FROM THE CIA

The Central Intelligence Agency's Publications Review Board has reviewed the manuscript for this book to assist the authors in eliminating classified information, and poses no objection to publication. This review, however, should not be construed as an official release of information, confirmation of its accuracy, or an endorsement of the authors' views.

To Jean
We miss your smiles and sense of humor

Mama? Where are we going?
What are all the suitcases for?
You said: darling, we're leaving for America,
Sweden and Finland,
The Netherlands and Norway,
Thailand and Germany, too.
Watch your brother for me while I pack,
won't you?

Excerpt from *"Eulogy for Eva G."*
by her Daughter
September 1998

TABLE OF CONTENTS

ACKNOWLEDGMENTS

We want to thank all the women who have so generously given of their time, energy, tears, and laughter. It was not always easy. Many had never spoken of some of these experiences. They had never talked of whom they worked for or what they had done. Their families, friends, and children often did not know. Now their anonymous voices can be heard, always within the bounds of security. A special thank you is due:

To all the women who contributed to this book. Without you it would not have become a reality.

To all the women who did not contribute, we hope this inspires you to express yourself, if only to a friend.

To those unnamed, who will recognize themselves in these stories. Just smile with the memories.

To Erin, the child of a spy, who first suggested that we have a lunch, invite some women, feed them some food and wine, and record it all.

To Madame Sathorn, who always believed it was *our* book.

To Austin Goodrich, our editor and friend, spy and freelance writer, who believed in these two broads when all we felt was stark terror.

To our husbands, James and William, who believed in us from the very start. We appreciate your patience, support, words of encouragement, and love.

To our children, Deborah and Christopher.

To the Central Intelligence Agency, thanks for the memories.

INTRODUCTION

London-Paris-Bangkok-Hong Kong-Berlin-Manila-Tokyo
Addis Ababa-Moscow-Warsaw-Vienna-Saigon

It all started at a Chinese luncheon in Langley. We got together as two kindred souls, old friends from the Central Intelligence Agency (CIA). We reminisced about places we had lived and people we had known. We were both at a new chapter in our lives and searching for a beginning. We'd had thousands of days and nights of wonderful experiences during our years overseas with the CIA and had accompanied our husbands to exotic and dangerous places. We had something to say. It had not been done before. What a marvelous idea! And that is how this all began.

We started gathering names from old address books; memories prompted us to think of others. We found women in cities and countries around the globe. We interviewed women who came to share our excitement. Some had new names and new husbands. Some were widows. Some did not want to talk to us, and we respected that. Others felt they had nothing to share, perhaps a result of those lonely nights and days when they could not disclose themselves to others. Some memories stay buried in the recesses of our hearts. But this was the beginning of numerous luncheons, afternoon teas, telephone calls, e-mails, conversations, and then, this book.

We were not women soaring on the coattails of our men. We brought ourselves to these adventures. We saw, we read, we heard, we participated, we changed, and we grew. We looked back on these experiences, and we reflected on what we did and what it all meant.

We have, through these writings, allowed ourselves the luxury of reminiscing and an opportunity to consider the impact on our lives of the arcane environment in which we lived and served. Today we bring the wisdom of hindsight to these experiences. We have collected both cold facts and warm feelings, and now we reflect on them. We hope we are wiser for having done this. A crusty old case officer in Danang once told one of the authors: "You will have experiences which you would neither buy for a nickel nor sell for a million dollars." We respectfully submit that he was wrong: We paid dearly for our experiences, and they are not for sale at any price.

These are our stories. We, the wives, former wives, and children of CIA employees. We have talked among ourselves for many years—at the Majestic Hotel in Saigon and the Ritz in Paris, at the tiny Italian restaurant in Addis Ababa and the Peninsula in Hong Kong, on China Beach in Danang and the Costa Del Sol, in a safe house in Rio de Janeiro and in a hut by the side of the road. Perhaps you leaned over toward the next table in a restaurant in Langley, Virginia, once upon a time, to try and hear the conversation. Like life overseas, the stories are exciting, pathetic, joyful, and sad. They are believable and unbelievable. They are all true. We have served our country, sometimes in the quiet of the night, sometimes in searing sunlight. We have been behind the scenes and on the front pages of every newspaper in the world. If there was a war, we went. If there was a coup, we were evacuated. We have slipped and fallen, lied and fabricated, understood and been misunderstood. Our common thread: a deep respect for the CIA. It is our agency, and these are our lives. So, fasten your seatbelts! We wish you a wonderful journey through the adventures of SPIES' WIVES.

YOU KNOW
YOU ARE A CIA DEPENDENT WHEN . . .

The "Farm" does not bring thoughts of Grandpa's in Wisconsin but of a place near Williamsburg, Virginia.

Your husband tells you they are "sweeping" the house and no one shows up with a broom.

Your husband said he was off training guerrillas, and you realized he was not going to the zoo.

You realize that "making a pass" isn't about flirting.

You look for bugs in telephones and not flour.

Your husband has worked for three different organizations at the last three stations you were assigned to.

You start to believe you really do work for the State Department!

When you hear the word "recruitment" you don't think of a football team but a potential agent.

A neighbor tells you that your husband's car has been parked in a hotel parking lot for six hours and you really believe he had an "agent meeting."

Your spouse tells you he's going on TDY and will be home in two weeks and you mark his arrival for two months later.

Your husband tells you he's going on a trip and can't tell you where and you don't even wonder why.

You are told you must leave the country quickly and you are gone in the middle of the night.

"The Funny Farm" is a building in Langley, Virginia, and not an insane asylum.

The chief of station says they need you and you take a job as a "Contract Wife" for $4.00 an hour.

You always carry Lomatil in your cosmetic bag.

You drink only bottled water and Coke without ice.

You wash all your lettuce in Chlorox before you eat it.

You buy enough toilet paper for a year whenever you go to the supermarket.

Someone told you your father has contributed to world peace and you wonder how that could be true when he sold tractors for International Harvester.

Being "under cover" does not conjure up pictures of snuggling under a Laura Ashley comforter.

You are dining in a third-world restaurant and begin to think of the roach as a condiment.

SPIES' WIVES

Chapter I

FASTEN YOUR SEAT BELTS

Life overseas for Spies' Wives was very exciting, very boring, and sometimes frightening. We left some of ourselves behind in each post. Tragically, for some of us, we buried babies in distant lands and lost husbands through divorce and death. We came home older, wiser, and often jaded. Then came a new assignment, and the excitement started all over again. No matter how many times we packed up, resettled and reoriented ourselves to a new place, the adrenaline would start to flow again. New cultures, languages, targets, agents, political situations, dangers to conquer. That was probably the secret to our lives abroad. Starting over and loving it. You might think us just like any other government employee and his or her family overseas. But there was, and still is, one major difference: We could never reveal the true reason for our assignments overseas or the exact nature of our business. We seldom shared specifics, even with fellow CIA employees; compartmentation was a necessary part of espionage.

We often had only an outdated post report to find out what was needed in our new post. Some posts required shipping extra canned goods, diapers, and clothing for children's growing needs. Just imagine trying to guess how many diapers one would need for an infant. It was an overwhelming task, but we did it. Added to this was the fact that the agency really would have preferred not to have officers married. "If we wanted case officers to have wives, we would have issued them one!" said one senior agency employee.

When we began collecting stories for this book, we found a serious reluctance on the part of many women to share their experiences or reveal a lot of themselves to the world. So many years had been spent in the background and hiding the truth that it was painful to come out of the closet, so to speak. Some women could not bring themselves to recount their fears and sorrows. Some did. A generation that will never be again. Things have changed and are more progressive within the agency today. Married and overseas with a career of one's own is now a reality. We hope we've paved the way for much of the progress that has been made. Join us along this journey through the dark alleys and silent rooms of CIA life overseas.

She was flying upcountry on the Air America Courier flight to her new home. She glanced at the information sheet she had picked up at the Embassy. It read "In Danang one finds many things reminiscent of back home. Fishing and beaches equal to those of Florida. The French style restaurants recalling memories of New Orleans. You will find a home away from home in the U.S.O. and Special Services to provide facilities for relaxation. Yes, you will enjoy Danang." How right they were, but for all the wrong reasons. This was her first tour overseas. She fastened her seat belt and prepared for the ride.

From the Post Report for Danang 1964

The Emperor Who Waved

"Marry me," my wasband (former husband) said, "and I'll take you on a fabulous honeymoon through Europe." This is my man! Yes! Conveniently, he forgot to mention that the end of the trip would be Addis Ababa, Ethiopia. Where? Africa? Ethiopia? So off we went—me, a twenty-four-year-old who had never been north of New York City or south of Florida and he, a brand-spanking-new CIA Career Trainee (CT), Class of '66.

The minute the plane landed and doors opened, we knew we were some place other than Mom's kitchen. The stench of the place was so startling it took your breath away—a mixture of beriberi spice, human waste, and general garbage. There is no such thing as trash removal in Ethiopia. Off to the Hotel Ethiopia, the only hotel (and I use that word "hotel" loosely) in the city (and I use the word "city" loosely), where the next morning we awakened itching and scratching from Ethiopian fleas, which were in the mattress by the millions. Husband was whisked off to the office while I was left to my own devices to entertain myself for eight hours. No TV, no newspaper, no room service, so I mustered/gathered/summoned up my courage, opened the door, and ventured outside. At once I was surrounded by what seemed like hundreds of begging children and lepers with various forms of disfigurement. The children were chanting "no mother, no father" and the begging lepers were removing various dirty rags from their deformities to shove them in my face. Not a pretty sight! After realizing the situation I was in, with no help around and being pushed, shoved, jostled, and touched by people with diseases, I ran screaming into the lobby, where the bellboy announced, "Not safe for you, Missy!" Now he tells me.

After a month of living in the hotel, we moved into our own house, which was surrounded by twelve foot walls with broken glass and barbed wire lining the top. The wall kept out humans, but the monkeys roamed freely and the vultures would perch on top waiting for something or someone to die. I decided not to be the next meal! Many months later, after we became acclimated to the post and often ventured out into the countryside, we would see vultures by the hundreds sitting around dying donkeys and cows, waiting for them to lie down.

Our maid spoke five languages but still had the habit of saying "yes" to everything, even when she clearly did not understand what we were saying or asking her to do. Saying yes was a way of "saving face," which was a big priority, and rather than admit that they did not understand, the servants would just let you think that they did. Before we had left for Ethiopia, we had read the State Department Post Report, which told us to ship in bulk any supplies that we would need for our two-year tour. A hair setting lotion, Get Set, was something I could not do without so I shipped a case over in the household effects. After several months, I realized that I could not find my Get Set until one day I happened to come home early and found the maid with a bottle of Get Set in one hand and a rag in the other. She thought Get Set was Windex and had been using it on our windows for months.

The office in Addis Ababa was located at the top of the one good road in the city. The Emperor's palace was at the bottom of the same road, and every day, Haile Selassie, Lion of Judah, would ride up the hill in what looked like a two-block-long Rolls Royce to the top of the mountain for prayers. He would make this trip each day at noon just as we were on our way home for the two-hour lunch break. When the Emperor passed by, we had to get out of our cars and bow. Daily we encountered the Emperor on his way to prayers; and daily we would get out of our cars to bow. After a while, I would peek up as I bowed and give the Emperor a little wave. He in turn would give me a little smile and a small wave.

We were permitted to use the Emperor's weekend

retreat, and so several times a month, a group of us would drive over the dusty rutted roads to Galila Palace where there was an actual swimming pool. Before swimming, however, we would have to clean out the thousands of bugs that lived on top of the water. Often the Emperor was also at the palace, occupying one wing, while we had the rest of the palace to ourselves. Many times he, surrounded by bodyguards, would come down to the pool to watch us have fun in the water. When we spotted him and scrambled out of the water, he would give us a shy smile and a "carry-on" wave. He loved Americans. The Emperor would leave his retreat at about three in the afternoon to return to Addis. He had two guard cars ahead of his Rolls Royce, which was followed by another guard car. We Americans, frequently drunk from our afternoon at the swimming pool, would follow behind, so the caravan was a very long one. The Emperor threw clean white cotton cloth out of the window to the villagers, who would make themselves new *shammas* (native dress robes) out of the material. We Americans wearing plastic pith helmets threw candy and beer cans out our windows. The villagers loved cans of any sort and used them for many things. Nothing like the versatile can. Nothing like drunk Americans! No wonder these people never understood us.

Being a newlywed in Ethiopia definitely had its drawbacks, especially if you did not know how to cook. We lived on ungarnished Spam and Dinty Moore beef stew for most of our meals. I swore after that tour that I would never again eat either of these delicacies, and I never have. The commissary was one room about the size of a double garage. Most of the time the shelves were empty except for flour, which came in twenty-five pound bags and had to be debugged before you could use it. Fresh meat was flown in from Kenya once every six weeks, and the choices were usually only huge frozen fish or water buffalo roasts. Very tough! During our second year, a new ambassador arrived who actually felt sorry for the "troops" and had a load of fresh turkeys flown in for Thanksgiving. He invited all the American personnel to the residence for a good old-fashioned home-cooked dinner, and since most of us had not had turkey and all the trimmings for eighteen months, we pigged out. That night, every one of us got ptomaine poisoning to the point where we prayed for a quick death! The ambassador, who also got sick, called everyone to explain that the servants had stuffed the turkeys the night before and had left them out on the counters overnight!

We went on to other assignments, but I will always remember this one as the one where an Emperor waved at me every day.

Along for the Ride

When I was asked to share some of my stories of life inside the highest intelligence organization in the world, it brought back a flood of memories that I could not control. When I started to write them down on paper, I could not write fast enough.

It started thirty-four years ago the first week in September, with my first international flight, and only the second flight of my life, to Bonn, Germany. This was the land of the killers of European Jews (my mother had told me the stories of the Holocaust), and I was frozen with fear! Everything I had was on this massive jet. Three precious little boys, ages three months, two years, and five years, and my best friend, my husband of six years—a brand-spanking-new JOT (Junior Officer Trainee) barely out of spy school! I had packed mounds of cloth diapers (no paper ones in those days), baby lotion, pacifiers, rattles, baby clothes, and all the other paraphernalia for the baby; plus toys, books, and other distractions to keep the older two happy during the long flight. Under my seat was a box marked Colt. 45—an anniversary gun given to my husband by his father as a going away gift with the warning, "Ya never know when you're going to need this, son!" I was twenty-four years old and in total shock. I silently cried, trying to keep my face turned so that my husband and my children could not see the tears sliding down my face. I was petrified that we would crash into the Atlantic, since the plane was bouncing all over the sky and we had been advised to keep our seatbelts tightened. "Maybe this is normal," I thought, but how was I going to live through all this? I was scared. How would I cope? But I knew that I had to be brave for the sake of my babies and my husband. After all, he would take care of everything; he always had.

He had the college education. I didn't, and he knew what was best for us, or so he told me. I was just along for the ride!

Arriving in Bonn to pouring rain and gray skies, we were stuffed into two taxis for the long ride to our hotel. I began to think that we had no clothes on because of all the stares and gawkings from the Germans. I could hear the word "Amerikanish" said with distaste and disgust. I felt intimidated and embarrassed. Fear gripped my throat—maybe we were not supposed to be here. Had we done something wrong? Were we going to be arrested and taken away somewhere? Was the war really over—did they still gas people? All these thoughts were running through my mind until I thought that I would go mad! I drew my precious bundles closer to me. No one spoke to me except my husband who fortunately also spoke German. He told me that everything was fine, and I finally began to relax a little. I became fascinated with how different everything looked—the gingerbread houses just like the ones in the Hansel and Gretel story, the cars that went very, very fast, and flowers everywhere. My God, I was so naive and had so much to learn. It was only the beginning!

It's Not Easy Being Green

As a young working wife with two small children, the anticipation of an overseas assignment seemed like a blessing in disguise. A wonderful chance to see the world at Uncle Sam's expense, to be able to stay home with the kids and save money for a "rainy day." All of these goals were accomplished with a few deviations, disappointments, and some embarrassing moments.

At our first posting in Manila during the Vietnam War, I made many discoveries and my share of mistakes. I had never flown before and had never been away from my family for more than two weeks at a time. I had no idea of what lay ahead for me.

The twenty-hour flight from Washington, DC, was broken up with a five-day stay in Honolulu. This short vacation was wonderful after the hectic time of packing, getting our shots, and saying goodbye to our loved ones. It also helped with the jet lag caused by crossing twelve time zones. After a relaxing time in Honolulu, we flew what seemed like halfway around the world, and arrived in Manila in the middle of the night. What a shock! There was a burned-down airport with only a runway and a makeshift terminal. Four hundred Filipinos greeted us at the plane—they were looking for jobs as ayahs (nannies), gardeners, and drivers. Arriving with a one-year-old son and a three-year-old daughter put my family in demand. Everyone was pressing forward trying to touch my daughter's blonde hair—it is supposed to be good luck, so I was asked by the officer who met us not to be offended by it. I would take care of my own children; I did not need a nanny. I managed to survive the first week of adapting to the temperature, the surroundings, and my new status as an overseas wife. It soon became apparent that, given our social schedule, I would need to hire a nanny, and while I was at it, I needed a maid and a gardener, too. I hired and fired several before we found a staff that we liked and felt comfortable with.

Our first command performance was a welcome party for new arrivals, which was held at the ambassador's residence a week after we arrived. Fortunately, I had purchased a long tropical flowing dress in Hawaii that seemed appropriate attire for this party. I will never forget the look on our children's faces as we left them in the very capable hands of the newly hired nanny I was never going to have! So much for resolve. The embassy driver picked us up and delivered us to the residence. I had arrived! Small-town girl no more, I thought as the car door was opened by the white uniformed servant. If my family could see me now!

As we mingled with some of the people we had met at the embassy, I was overwhelmed with the luxurious house and its grand furnishings. Embassy cocktail parties could be overwhelming, especially to a young wife new to overseas life. You stand around waiting for anyone to come and talk to you, and you get the feeling that you are standing there naked and everyone is staring at you because you have no friends. I had very little experience with drinking, so I felt intimidated when the houseboy approached to take my drink order. I cannot remember to this day what I ordered, but whatever it was, it gave me the courage to move away from my husband's side and mingle with some of the other wives. I joined a conversation about where these ladies had lived. Oh, this one I could handle. One of the more seasoned women in this group had just arrived in the Philippines from Vienna. I got enough courage to speak: "Oh, really, I lived near Vienna." Now that I had her attention, she asked me where I had lived. "Alexandria," I replied. "Vienna, Austria, my dear, not Vienna, Virginia," she cried, looking down her nose at me. I said no more that evening.

I have been in many other places and have attended countless cocktail parties and am no longer green. Since that day I have always tried to seek out the women who have felt naked at cocktail parties, and I have not given them a geography test. I am no longer an agency wife and do not travel as I once did. I saw parts of the world I never imagined in my wildest dreams, got to stay home with my children during their formative years, saved some money for a rainy day and, thanks to the efforts of other agency wives, I can now enjoy a substantial allotment based on my ex-husband's retirement that all former spouses now get.

All in all, a marvelous experience.

Sawadii

Our male servant of five years was dressed in white carrying a silver tray and crystal glasses and serving the best PX champagne. Madame (as the servants called me) was dressed in black-and-white hot pants and a long black coat with knee-high laced-up patent leather boots. Master was in his Mao jacket of Thai silk, and our five-year-old son in a normal pair of shorts and sneakers with the servants constantly running around after him with a Kleenex to wipe his face. Oh, a picture to behold. Madame was being briefed for the last time on what her child ate for breakfast, never having had to feed him for the past five years. It was the VIP room at Don Muang International Airport on the day of departure from Bangkok after two tours. Thai and American friends were crowded around, and tears, laughter, and scotch were abundant. It was to be a grand trip home—flight to Tokyo, short drive to Yokohama, overnight at a hotel, and board the ship by noon for a twenty-one-day cruise on the President Cleveland to San Francisco. All the tickets had been purchased, sea freight sent well ahead to the ship, and soon it was time to leave. The Thai immigration officer checked the diplomatic passports for departure clearance. One hour to go before we bid farewell to "the land of smiles."

Two Thai officers entered the party room. "Sir, we regret to inform you that you do not have a visa for Japan. If you enter Japan from an airport and depart from another location, you must have a visa. This is not considered a transit stop. You do not have a visa, and we cannot let you on this flight to Japan." Surely you must be kidding? We have a ship to catch. How could the travel section at the embassy overlook this? Guess what! They did. Plan B does not exist, but we must find one.

It is Saturday and we cannot get from Bangkok to Tokyo tomorrow in time to make the ship. We need a Japanese visa. This flight stops in Hong Kong. We are getting geographically closer if we go to Hong Kong. We, minus our baggage, decide to stop in Hong Kong. But the wig box goes with us. Tickets must be changed to read stop in Hong Kong. Luggage will go to Tokyo. Our office in Hong Kong must be notified to meet the plane, get us a place to sleep, contact the Japanese consulate, and plead with the Japanese visa officer to give us a visa on Sunday morning at dawn. Tickets are hastily changed. A car comes to the door of the party room to take us to the airplane at the last minute. Tears are shed and we get into the car. Ooops, no kid. The baby amah and our son are in the bathroom crying. Run to the bathroom and grab our son, *Sawadii* (good-bye) to everyone, limo to stairs of airplane, and down the aisle to our seats as all the annoyed passengers gaze at us as if we had never traveled before.

Pilot radios messages to Hong Kong. No one there to meet us. Take a cab to the hotel closest to the airport and drop on the beds. Phone rings. Case officer was at a party and just got the immediate cable, wants us to stay with them so that they can continue to try to get in touch with the Japanese consulate. Must get there at 6 A.M. because the flight to Tokyo leaves at 7:30 A.M. Okay. Grab our son, grab the wig box, put on the patent leather boots, take the Star Ferry across the harbor, hop into a cab, and go to our friend's mid-level flat. We are greeted with much welcome. How about going out for Chinese food? Why not. We don't have anything else to do. No luggage—that went to Tokyo. Leave the kid with another baby amah—he thinks they are all his mother anyway—and off we go for a good Chinese meal. I could find that restaurant twenty years later. We start phoning. Sorry, all visa officers are at a cocktail party as it is a Japanese holiday. Finally, Mr. Hirosomoshitoto is on the phone at ten P.M. with forty scotches under his belt. *So sorry—we don't issue visas on Sunday morning at 6 A.M.* Why not?

Look mister—remember Pearl Harbor? You owe us one! *Okay, I will meet you at 6 A.M. as a special favor to the American people.*

Return to the flat where we fall into a deep sleep and dream of lost vacations and horizons. Up at 5 A.M. Same kid, same clothes, same hot pants, and same Mao jacket! Now this gets complicated. Madame and child must take tickets to airport, explain to ticket counter lady that Master is coming with visas and passports and they must wait for us. Surely four hundred passengers on a jumbo jet will wait for us to get on. Only luggage we have at this point is Madame's wig box, and kid is carrying that. Master gets driver from consulate to take him to Japanese visa office. Visas get issued. Many thanks and bows. Madame and kid are at airport. Kid and wig case have been on the luggage belt twice and been pulled off at the last minute before being shipped out to oblivion. Madame and child both stare out the window looking for a badly wrinkled Thai silk Mao jacket that finally runs through the door. Ticket agent calls the plane. *Hold it—here comes Mr. Mao, Ms. Leather Boots, kid, and wig box.*

Car meets us at door and with lightning speed we are hurled to the steps of the airplane. We run down the aisle to our seats receiving hard looks from another group of travelers. Three seats all together, wig box in between. Sit down, peace at last. Wrong!! Kid throws up. All over seat. All passengers in front and behind are sprayed. Blankets are pushed in place, and 4711 perfume is sprayed everywhere to cover up the smell. God, they love us!

The pilot has radioed Tokyo. Meet us and drive us to Yokohama to board the ship. We have exactly two hours to make it. *Glad to do it.*

The young support officer was told to look for two adult diplomats with a five-year-old child. He ignored the three who got off the plane that were obviously from some English circus and had been up all night. But there were no other Caucasians with a child. Could it be? You got it. We thanked him profusely, retrieved our luggage that had been sent the day before, and got in the car to drive to Yokohama. One problem. They had no office drivers in Tokyo, and our support officer friend had never been to Yokohama!! Why didn't the office send. . . don't ask . . Well, we got lost, of course. But finally, on the horizon, there she is! The most grand and glorious sight to behold—a ship that says "American President Lines." We have fifteen minutes to find our luggage on the dock, a task eased by the fact that it was the only trunk left.

We made it! It was the most wonderful cruise we have ever had. Our bar bill was $800. The wig box was tossed overboard on the first day out and I never wore hot pants again. But about that Mao jacket. . .

Unpaid Servitude

I had spent two weeks in a training course for wives going overseas where I had listened, taken notes about cultural differences and proper decorum, laughed at language faux pas. It never occurred to me to worry. It sounded so exciting, so fascinating! I returned to Langley one day in time to meet the new ambassador to our assigned post and the chief and deputy chief of Africa Division.

It was the first time for me to meet the chief of Africa Division, whose reputation and notoriety preceded him. He asked what I had learned that day. I told him that I had been informed that my "performance" could not be used in my husband's efficiency report unlike in previous years. For example, if the ambassador's wife said jump, I no longer had to ask, "How high?" The chief of Africa Division looked at me and very dryly remarked, "But remember, my dear, your husband does not work for State!"

And so began a twenty-seven-year stint of "unpaid servitude" to God, country, husband, and the "office." Fortunately for my family, the ambassador had asked my husband to wait until his orders came through before we would leave for the post. Four days after we were originally scheduled to arrive in Khartoum, this noble statesman and the deputy chief of mission (DCM), who had been serving as the charge d'affaires, were victims of the Black September reign of terror. They were captured, tortured, and executed. Both of these men died in a country they loved, having served previously in the Sudan and returning for second tours.

Two months after these men were slain, we arrived at post and were brought to our new quarters. My first reaction to seeing the house was "been here, seen this before." It had been the residence of another agency officer years earlier who had shown us the slides from his tour and included pictures of his house, the city, and his elephant hunt. The house had enchanted me, the city shots had depressed me, and the elephant kill made me head for the nearest basin. We were told that this house had been the favorite of the DCM's. I could not understand why, when we invited people in after they had been kind enough to take me shopping or had come to pick us up for some function, they all declined. Then one day a Marine and two wives who had taken me "commissary" shopping agreed to come in. The Marine commented that the "floor is still warm" and I found out that no one wanted to come in because the living and dining rooms supposedly had been used as the temporary morgue after the slayings. The powers that be would never confirm or refute this information.

I went to our first tour with eyes and mind opened, but I did not see all and I comprehended little (thank God). I became the "hostess with the mostest" on four continents. I served lasagna and beef burgundy and pizza and homemade tortellinis to "tinker, tailors, soldiers, and mostly spies." I met emirs and princes, chieftains and directors. I fed the masses of TDYers and the throngs of servants' children. I hope they enjoyed the food prepared by an "Italian Mother," who as the saying goes, never totally lets go of her children, her recipes, or her kitchen. Our cooks always had to remember that there was a higher authority in the kitchen—me! During our postings in Europe, I was the chief cook and bottle washer because few families could afford the luxury of hiring a cook there. We laughed, we cried they were the best of times, they were the worst of times.

In retrospect, I think of how fortunate I have been to experience the joys of meeting and learning about other cultures. I mourn the loss of many friends I have been fortunate enough to meet whose faces are forever emblazoned on my soul, but the memories of our shared experiences fill my heart to the brim.

First Tour

My husband came home that first September we were in Washington and told me that we would be leaving for Germany in late November. At first I was so excited—as a child, I had always dreamed of going to exotic places. It took about a week for reality to set in. We had just moved to Washington in July and now, in less than six months, we would not only be moving again, but also leaving the United States. Scary! So while I wrestled with the thoughts of being lonely and so far from home, the other part of me said, "Wow! You are going to be living in Europe!"

This is how all of our tours were—the excitement of living abroad coupled with the loneliness and separation from family and friends. Our husbands go into their offices and they are right at home; their environment has changed very little, while ours is challenged with trying to find where to shop, how to communicate with people in languages that we have only studied for a short time, and, more importantly, help our children adjust to new schools, new neighborhoods, and new friends. But I digress.

Before I knew it, pack-out day arrived. My only experience with packing out had been our move to Washington, which was not the same because all of our belongings were shipped. Packing out for an overseas tour is completely different. It is traumatic even for the seasoned traveler; but for a novice, it is a nightmare. It was really difficult for me to believe that if I made a mistake and left something behind, I would not see it again for at least two years. So here I was, trying to sort for sea shipment, air shipment, and storage. I was told that I could ship 3500 pounds by sea. As I stood in our apartment, I tried to imagine what 3500 pounds looked like! I tried weighing things, but quickly gave up on that.

The air shipment was easier because it consisted of our clothing, some kitchen utensils, and dishes. I made so many mistakes, like not putting our tree ornaments in the air shipment (went in the sea shipment, which did not arrive until late February) or putting my daughter's toys in storage. Like she was going to play with them when she returned for college! Or putting my daughter's winter clothing in the sea shipment—again, when I look back on it today, I wonder how I could have been so stupid, but this is from experience gained from seven overseas assignments.

Added to all this stress was the fact that most of these pack-outs were going on at the same time. I tried to keep the different shipments in separate rooms, but somehow things still got mixed up. Thank God for the PX—I could purchase new winter clothes for my daughter. Needless to say, by the time the sea shipment arrived, she had a very extensive wardrobe!

I had borrowed my neighbor's roasting pan to take the food from our freezer to our neighbor. The packers called me to another room, I put the pan down, and voila, it was packed for storage! It was gone and already loaded onto the truck. I bought the roaster from my neighbor and had the top packed into storage too. I still have the pan, and every time I look at it, I have to laugh about how I came to own it.

The trucks had barely pulled away and I was cleaning up the apartment when my husband came home and informed me that I was on what is called a "medical hold." I asked my husband what that meant and he told me that I could not leave until the doctors gave me approval to go. He and our daughter would be leaving on Saturday but there was a very good chance that I would not be with them. I had been under medical treatment for a thyroid condition for more than two years and had noted that in my medical history statement. No one paid any attention to that until the time came for the doctors to sign off on the travel orders. Suddenly it became an issue.

This was Wednesday afternoon at 5 P.M.; the next day was Thanksgiving, and how were we going to get this resolved? And more importantly, where would I be living while it was being resolved? Our car had been shipped, our sea and air shipments were on trucks going to the port of Baltimore, and the household effects had been taken to storage. I had no car, no furniture, and no apartment because we had broken the lease. It made no difference because I would have had nothing to put in it anyway. The earliest that I could see the doctors would be Friday morning.

I was so upset! Our daughter was only six at the time and she would be going to a strange land while her mother was still in Washington? At the same time, I had no place for either of us to stay. We had filled out our medical information shortly after we arrived in Washington—how could this have happened? Why did it take so long for someone to read the file? It made no sense. Later, I discovered that my experience was not unique. It seems that dependents are way down on the totem pole until it comes time for the medical staff to sign off. Then suddenly, all hell breaks loose.

We had borrowed a car to use until our departure, but of course my husband needed it to go to the office. He had to be there early, and my appointment to see the doctors was not until 9 A.M. I could not go earlier because we thought that there would be no place for me to wait. We were so new to the agency that we really had no idea of what we could or could not do. Fortunately my neighbor loaned me her car, and so on Friday morning, I went for the first time to the building! At that time, there was no sign on the highway to tell you where to turn—if you did not know where it was, you did not belong there. I was shaking as I drove onto the compound. After all, I had been told never to talk about my husband being with the agency so I had tried never to think about it. When I got to the guard's kiosk, I was not even certain that I should give him my name. What was really crazy about the whole exercise was while I was stopped at the kiosk, my neighbor's husband drove through and saw me in his wife's car. He never mentioned it, and neither did I when I saw him later. I finally got up to the front of the building. There is nothing more imposing than agency headquarters, because of the mystique and knowledge that only a chosen few are allowed in. I still get goosebumps each and every time I go through the front doors. I met with the doctors and then spent the rest of the day hoping and praying that I would be cleared and would be able to get on the plane with my family. Finally the clearance came through, and we were on our way.

Munich, even in the mid-sixties, bore some scars of the war. I remember that the city looked gray—drab and gray. We took a taxi to McGraw Kaserne where we reported in at the gate and were given a set of keys to an apartment we would stay at during our processing. I had learned from someone that McGraw Kaserne had been the Gestapo headquarters during the war, and it was really eerie to see some railroad tracks that ended within the Kaserne. Years later we went back to Munich and went to McGraw again and it still looked gray.

We were very happy to leave for our new home in Berchtesgaden in the Alps. The office had sent one of the officers to pick us up, and so on a beautiful, sunny day, we were off on our first adventure on a German autobahn. We could see the Alps in the distance with their snow-covered peaks, like a scene out of *The Sound of Music*. We sped past mad King Ludwig's castle at Chiemsee, and after driving through some lovely Bavarian villages, we arrived in Berchtesgaden, known the world over as the home of Hitler's Eagle's Nest. The chief invited us to dinner and we had to hire a baby-sitter. I asked the concierge at the hotel and he recommended a Frau Glogger. She arrived, a lovely woman with a winning smile. Our daughter felt comfortable with her, and so off we went to dinner. When we returned, I found empty beer bottles on the window sill. I was so angry because I could not believe that the babysitter would drink while she was caring for my daughter. I called the desk and told them about it, only to be told by the concierge that beer to a German is like cola to Americans. So much for my first culture shock.

Soon we moved into our apartment house, and the eerie echoes from the past persisted. The place had served as an SS officers' billet and casino. The apartment was lovely with a magnificent view of the Alps, but somehow the knowledge that it had been used by SS officers sort of took the charm off the place.

Our daughter started school and for the first few months, the tour was interesting. I learned enough German to be able to shop in the little stores that dotted the town. But about four months after we arrived, my husband left on TDY (temporary duty) elsewhere and he was gone for almost nine months. I tried to keep busy by reading the books at the US Army library, but with only a six year old for company, the loneliness got to me. Berchtesgaden was a recreation center for the Army, so there were very few families posted there and the few that were there were busy with their own lives. I felt like a fish out of water—alone and lonely. It soon became clear that my husband had to work in another city and would only return to Berchtesgaden for brief visits. I decided that if I had to live alone, I would rather live alone in the States where I had family and friends. I wrote to my husband of my intention, and he came home the following weekend to try to talk me out of my decision, but I was adamant.

I made arrangements to leave and notified the office that my daughter and I would be leaving. A few days later, there was a knock at the door. I opened the door and saw a man who identified himself as our local chief's boss. This meant absolutely nothing to me because we were so isolated from the other agency people that I had no idea who the chief's boss was. He informed me that I could not leave without his permission. I told him that I had purchased my own tickets and that he could not make me stay. After all, I was a citizen of the United States, and I believed that I could make my own decisions about my life. He told me that I would ruin my husband's career, but at the time, I was not concerned with that. I was only concerned that if I remained there alone, I would go mad and I did not think that would help my husband's career either.

My daughter and I flew home and we stayed with my mother while waiting for my husband to return to Washington. We were with my mother for nine months, and when my husband returned, he asked for a divorce. We eventually reconciled and my daughter and I joined him in Washington. It had been a very difficult first tour. We served seven more tours before retirement, and I enjoyed them all.

Sixth Cataract on the Nile

For New Year's, four couples traveled through the desert to the sixth cataract on the Nile, which, by the way, turned out to be a little water running over some boulders on one side of the river! After hours of trekking through miles and miles of flat sand, we came to the shores of the Nile where a few "mountains" stretched above the banks. There to our surprise stood a straw-covered lean-to held up by poles with a sign that read "Safari Club." We had a good chuckle until out of nowhere appeared the proprietor of the "club" asking for sixty pounds (about $150) for the use of the premises for the weekend. Luckily the USIS information officer was with us and he bargained the price down to twenty pounds. For this we got to use the lean-to for shade or parking and he would see that we were not disturbed by the children (what children?) and that our trash would be collected. Then he began cutting thorn tree branches to make a protective fence around our campground. The next morning I made a visit to the company loo, down over the cliff. I was still laughing about the "children" who were going to disturb us out here in the middle of nowhere when I glanced up from the throne to see about twenty pairs of eyes watching the lady on the box! They were, however, on the other side of the thorn tree barrier. Nonetheless, I wanted to get out of there as soon as possible.

There was a mountain or large hill that we were told had a beautiful view of the entire area—it was outside the camp, so it was fair game for the children. As we attempted to climb up one side of the hill, the little dears appeared and using sign language informed us that the route we were taking would lead to broken heads and they would lead us up a safer path. We followed them to the top—they were in rubber thongs, and we were in hiking boots (and panting hard). All the little hands went out for "baksheesh" but we told them no baksheesh until they led us down again.

At the time Kissinger was traveling the Middle East in hopes of bringing some peace and stability to the area. He was visiting Egypt, and as we descended the hill, the oldest boy asked my husband if he was British. "No, American," my husband answered. The boy's face lit up in recognition. "Oh, Henry Kissinger," gasped the child. "No." My husband said, who at twenty-eight and blonde, did not resemble our senior statesman at all. "Just his friend."

Later in the day, our host, the owner of the Safari Club, came to visit. Yes, the children stayed away and yes, each morning and evening the trash disappeared. Later everyone took a turn riding his very ornery looking camel, and in the end, I was convinced that I should do it just once. Unfortunately, the camel had had enough! As I started up onto the saddle, the camel got up and took off with me hanging half on/half off. My husband had a difficult time deciding if he should save me or get the Kodak moment! Finally, he and the other men corralled the disgusting little dromedary, but not before he had caused me much pain. I was bruised from one knee up around and down to the other knee. The next day our host returned with his donkey. "Maybe Madam would rather try my donkey." My response is unprintable.

Give Me Three Scotches

I was flying out of Tokyo into Manila after an emergency trip home in 1972. We were only an hour out of Tokyo when I, sitting in the window seat, noticed three islands below go by twice! I thought it was terribly odd to have three small islands like that in the Pacific Ocean so close together. The plane was full of Japanese except for a few Brits. I think I was the only American on board. I then noticed that the stewardesses (that is what they were called back then) were running up and down the aisles offering free drinks. So, I tapped the Brit in front of me and asked him if he thought anything was fishy about these free drinks. The people next to me only spoke Japanese, so I could not ask them. The Brit didn't think much about this until we saw smoke coming out of the left engine on our side! Lots of black smoke, lots of free drinks, and finally the captain came on to say we were turning around due to a slight malfunction. Slight malfunction? This was not a Shelly Berman record, for those of you who remember him. This was the real thing. The pilot said it would take about forty-five minutes to get back to Tokyo, so I figured I may as well get drunk if I was going to die. Would have liked to enjoy a few other pleasures but this Brit was not my type and the aisles were crowded. So we cleared the liquor cart just as the engine actually caught fire and had to be shut down. Three engines and still no land in sight. Then came the announcement to remove shoes (never could figure that one out, if I were going to walk on water, it would help to have some shoes). We were then ordered to please put heads on pillows. No need to tell me that since I was half in the bag anyway. In case you ever hear that there was no panic on the plane, don't believe it. I created a small riot all by myself. Finally we could see the lights of the airport. Nothing since has ever looked so fantastic as those landing lights. We landed on that white foam and had to go down the chutes, and as I neared the chute (I fear that I may have killed some people getting to the front), the woman ahead of me refused to jump into the chute which was about twenty-four inches from the side of the plane. I had to give her a boost on the butt, and off she shot with me close behind. Luckily, I had had enough alcohol to desensitize me because I really hit hard at the bottom.

The word was that they would put a new engine on and we could be off in a few hours or we could stay overnight in Tokyo. Hello, Tokyo!

Surprise! Surprise!

On our second visit to Bahrain, we found the Emir's beach—a beautiful private beach that the Emir allowed foreigners to use. My husband showed his diplomatic ID and the guards told him he could park anywhere. He pulled up right next to a vintage 1956 Chrysler Imperial in front of a beautiful villa with a pier out over the water. As we walked to the pier, a lovely little man approached us, wearing a white robe with the neck opened and papers stuffed in the pocket. He and my husband talked about the beautiful car and he asked where we were from. My husband told him he was posted in Riyadh. The man said "Oh, and we still don't have an American ambassador there." Picking up on the "we," my husband asked if he were Saudi. "Oh no," answered the slight gentleman, "I am the Emir of Bahrain." We thanked him profusely for allowing us to use his beach. He asked if we would like coffee. We were shocked and embarrassed and said that we did not wish to take up any more of his time and went off to find a spot on the beach. About an hour later, a servant came and sought us out, telling us that "the Emir would like you to have coffee," whereupon, out came bone china, sterling silver coffee service, juice and (I could swear) Sara Lee pound cake. We had met some friends from Riyadh on the beach and about three hours later, our banker friend said "Hey, I'm getting hungry—you want to ask the Emir what he has for lunch?" We laughed but just could not believe how down to earth and hospitable this head of state was.

She Just Kept Ironing

She sat with her back to the bedroom door holding the gun that her husband had given her. He had brought it home from the office "just in case." Moments earlier, she had been downstairs in the newly rented house where she had lived for just four days. The maid was ironing in the servants' quarters when she heard gunfire across the street. People milled around outside the gate. She urged the maid to come upstairs with her, but the woman just kept ironing. The gunfire got louder, and she finally ran upstairs to the dark bedroom, got the gun and sat on the floor just waiting. An hour went by and nothing happened. Finally she managed to get upright and walk downstairs. She learned from the neighbor that five people had been killed across the street. Catholics fighting Buddhists. She glanced out back and the maid was still there, still ironing. Just one week ago she had been at John's Pizza Parlor in Norwalk, Connecticut. This was her first tour overseas.

Saigon 1964

From Washington to Udornthani

What do you do when you have always led a rather public life? By that I mean you are used to the perks that go with working for a very senior member of the United States Congress and you were brought up in the household of a high-ranking United States government official living many years in Latin America, but you marry someone whose job must remain a secret and you need to keep a low profile. It was an adjustment for me. Still, I would not change a thing; well, perhaps a few, but not many.

I met my husband-to-be at a dinner party in late February and married him on St. Patrick's Day. I had been a single parent working on Capitol Hill for many years, and now my daughter and I were on our way to Bangkok, where my husband was assigned. We arrived in the middle of the night. I had never seen such traffic.

We had decided that we wanted to have children right away so before I left the United States, I talked with someone who had lived in Bangkok and had gotten the name of three Thai doctors who had degrees from American medical schools. I met with one, Dr. Olarn, and really liked him. His wife was also a doctor, a pediatrician, so I was all set. As it so happened, Olarn's wife was expecting at the same time as I was; they had two boys and were hoping for a girl. Since we already had a daughter, we thought that a boy would be nice. Well, Olarn had another boy and we had a little girl. Olarn came into my room and asked if I thought that anyone would notice if we switched babies! Right!

During my pregnancy, I noticed that Thais would come up to me on the street and touch my stomach and smile. It had to be a friendly gesture, because the Thais are the happiest, nicest, and kindest people in the world.

I finally asked Olarn about this touching of the stomach, and he replied as he put his hand on my stomach, "If the baby moves, it brings good luck to me, and I am playing Poker tonight!"

When we brought our precious little baby girl home, we fixed a special room off our bedroom for her. We could not believe what a great baby she was! She never awakened during the night. I would get up and check, and she would be sleeping away. When Baby Jennifer was about two weeks old, we went out to dinner at a friend's home and stayed out very late. When we got home, sleeping on the landing of the stairs leading to our bedroom was the number two maid, Sumien (the number two maid did the laundry, baby-sat, and whatever else the number one maid, usually the cook, told her to do). The next day I asked our number one, Amala, why Sumien was sleeping on the floor. She informed me Sumien slept on the floor every night so she could feed baby Jennifer during the night and not disturb Master's sleep!

It was right about this time that we were informed we would be transferred to Udornthani, Udorn for short, in Northeast Thailand for the remainder of our tour. Udorn was not exactly the garden spot of the world, and we were upset that there would be no school for our oldest child. But transfers are transfers. One of the "senior" Agency wives informed me that we young officers' wives could not expect tours in Bangkok. We needed to get out in the "boonies" and "earn" our promotions. She told me this as she filled her PX basket with a dozen rolls of toilet paper—under a huge sign stating only two rolls per customer. The sign did not apply to her, she said, as she and her husband had seven children. Ah, yes, rank had its privileges. So we went to Udorn and my daughter took correspondence courses.

Moving up-country was really a blast. My husband sent our number one, Amala, up to Udorn to inspect the house he was having built, as there was no house available for us. At first she refused to go. We kept our fingers crossed, as I would be lost without her. Amala came back and informed us she would go because, "Madame cannot take care of Baby Jennifer."

I did not say one word. It was about this time that Amala said it was time to cut Baby Jennifer's eyelashes. I repeated what she said to make sure I heard correctly. Yes, I had. I asked Amala if Thai babies have their lashes cut, and she said, "Yes, to make them long and thick." I told Amala we did not need to do that to this American baby. However, I quickly added that I thought the idea of putting powder all over the baby was a good Thai custom. I suggested that we first discuss any new ideas before applying them to Baby Jennifer.

Finally we made the move to Udorn. Amala went ahead with her older brother, who lived with us off and on. We later found out he was a petty gangster in Bangkok, and when he was gone, he was back in jail. When he lived with us, he transported Marcy, our oldest daughter, to the Bangkok Pattana School in his three-wheeled *samlor*. He was very large for a Thai, and his pedi-cab was in good condition, so I was happy with the arrangement, not knowing of the man's extracurricular activities. Anyway, Marcy, Sumien, Baby Jennifer, my husband, and I drove to Udorn. The Thais had a strange and dangerous way of driving. If they wanted to pass, they did so no matter what was coming.

After a nerve-wracking ride, we arrived in Udorn and the house was lovely—Thai-style with the first floor, servants' rooms, kitchen, and big playroom all screened. Upstairs was the living room, dining room (with a dumbwaiter from the kitchen below), three bedrooms, and a bath. The dumbwaiter became Baby Jennifer's toy. Sumien rode in the dumbwaiter with Baby Jennifer while the yardboy, Dum-Dum, hauled them up and down. Small wonder that we still never heard Baby Jennifer cry, what with the servants spending all their time entertaining her.

Udorn was rather dangerous, so we also had an armed guard who lived with us. I called him Mr. Muscle, as he was a beautiful Thai ex-military policeman with a Colt .45 strapped on his belt. One day, when I was in the downstairs playroom with Baby Jennifer and Marcy, I found a medicine bottle with penicillin—the kind you stick a needle into and draw out a "dose." I got very upset and asked Amala, what this was all about. She informed me that the guard, Mr. Muscle, was "too cheap to go to 10-Baht alley for girl, he go to 5-Baht alley." She made him take shots so he would not get sick! She would not let him touch Baby Jennifer if he did not take the penicillin. So now, Baby Jennifer had a fifth adult at her beck and call, and she wasn't even one-year old!

We had a Dodge Dart convertible, and one day I needed to go to the beauty salon and buy some hair spray. Going to beautiful downtown Udorn, I put the top down and asked Mr. Muscle to go with me and Baby Jennifer. He could sit in the car while I went into the salon. I was not in the salon more than five minutes, and when I came out, the car was surrounded by a crowd of people in tattered clothing, and Mr. Muscle was standing up in the convertible with his gun in one hand and Baby Jennifer in the other. The assemblage were lepers who wanted to see the *farang* (Caucasian) baby. I made him sit down while I stood up with her and let them have a good look. They did not try to touch her. Mr. Muscle refused to put his gun away. I got into the car, handed Baby Jennifer to him, and drove off. Amala, suggested that it was not a good idea to take Baby Jennifer in the car any more. I agreed.

Our first Christmas in Udorn was memorable. We needed a tree for the children, so my husband and some Thais made us a tree. The Thais flew a helicopter into Laos, topped many pine trees, and we made a tree from three of them by sawing off limbs, drilling holes, inserting branches, and nailing the whole thing together. It was a very full tree. I had invited some pilots from the airbase for Christmas dinner. We could not find a whole turkey, but I did find some turkey breasts, which I stuffed with cornbread. We had a great time, proving that necessity was once again the mother of invention.

My husband, Marcy, and I decided we needed a vacation from Udorn, so we made reservations at the beach in Pattaya, even though it meant a hair-raising drive from Udorn. If we took Baby Jennifer, we would also have to take the servants, so we decided to leave her at home. Before we left, I took Baby Jennifer to the hospital at the air base because she had a slight case of the sniffles. A throat culture was taken and I was called and told the baby was fine, it was just sniffles, so away we went to the beach. Upon returning to Udorn, our agency "medic" met us and informed us Baby Jennifer had been very ill while we were gone. He told us that one morning as he went through the check point at the airbase gate, Amala was standing there, and when she recognized him, she jumped into his car and had him come to our house and take Baby Jennifer to the base hospital. Baby Jennifer's throat culture had been mixed up with someone else's, and she had a full-blown streptococcus infection! As her fever rose higher and higher, number one, number two, yard boy, guard, and petty gangster all made offerings to the king cobra that lived in the bamboo stand behind our house. Upon our return from the beach, a most elaborate altar had been set up for this cobra and Amala informed me that while the American doctor gave her medicine for Baby Jennifer, the offerings to the cobra had really cured her!

When it came time to leave Thailand, we were all sad. It had been the beginning of our married life together, and we had made so many wonderful friends, and had had so many wonderful experiences. To this day, we still cherish those friendships. They were new friendships for me, as many of these people had been stationed in Vietnam with my husband. When the cable first arrived in Bangkok that my husband would be arriving in April with "wife and child" to follow in July, a lot of money changed hands because they assumed the message was garbled and he could not possibly be married. They lost. Everyone should have a three-year honeymoon in Thailand!

Chapter II

THE HIDDEN SIDE OF LIFE OVERSEAS

Many women went overseas as "dependents of a person working for the US Government assigned abroad." They were well-educated and many had professional jobs of their own before their husbands chose the spook lifestyle. Stations were anxious to use their expertise and did so. The jobs were seldom ones that could be put on a resume. Wives contributed in numerous ways to the overall efforts of the CIA. What is truly remarkable is that wives did this with no training or even much knowledge of what the objective was. Unless we were employed as contract wives, we received no remuneration for our work. We were part of the husband/wife teams that spent untold hours "after hours" developing and recruiting potential agents.

" . . . I was caught up in the words spoken in the play, in the role and appearances, in responsibilities and expectations . . .," so reflected one of our writers.

Tradecraft, African Style

There was one Catholic church in Mogadishu, Somalia, that served as a site for brush (message-passing) encounters with the wife of a deep-cover agent. The kids and I would go to church and while exiting would walk through a dark vestibule where a "pass" would be made. Encrypted messages from her husband to mine would be secreted in the folds of some innocuous piece of paper or swatch of fabric. Other prime areas for *dead drops*, or passes, were in the butcher shop where she might pass the message to me inserted in a much-tested recipe in Italian, or at the "souk," the colorful marketplace, where vendors sold gold, ivory, and incense.

The agent's wife was a very dear friend who had moved to Mogadishu with her children. Once, in the middle of the night, my husband brought me to their home, for an emotional reunion. That was the only time we were able to talk to each other. If it was discovered that they were spying for the US, their lives could be in danger. Thereafter, our meetings were as strangers. Our eyes would lock in a knowing look of years of shared friendship of family ties that would not be severed by circumstances.

Friendships

One of the most difficult aspects of life overseas with the agency was an unwritten rule that wives were expected to seek out people of operational interest at cocktail parties and dinners. Most of us became quite proficient with a list of questions and developed a sixth sense about those who were potential assets, despite the fact that the agency did not believe that we had a "need to know." We were used as the spotters and assessors and then, after rapport had been established, the men would move in and take over. One of my friends described it as being taken out of the closet, dusted off, dressed up, sent out; and then, when the party was over, we were sent back into the closet.

Over the years, I had developed several friendships with the wives of men who were targets. At first I enjoyed meeting and getting to know these women. I have always been curious about the lives of women from other countries, and this was the perfect way to learn about them. We usually found a common bond with our children to start the dialogue. Quite often it took a long time for the women to feel comfortable enough to relax and really begin to develop a friendship. We had many lunches, dinners, teas, etc., before a friendship would be forged and we could enjoy our time together. One particular incident sticks out in my memory.

I had met a woman who was about my age and, despite a minor language barrier, we found that we had many similar interests and gradually became good friends. We spent many hours together, shopping, laughing, talking on the telephone—sharing our lives, or at least as much of our lives as we could. I could not tell her the real reason our friendship had started. My husband had reported my contact with this woman, and it was suggested that he meet her husband. This was my first experience with something like this, so I did not think that there was anything wrong with it. After all, it made perfect sense—she and I were friends and we wanted our husbands to become friends so that the four of us could do things together. Little did I know that once my husband started *developing* her husband, my time with her was limited. Eventually my husband pitched her husband (to work with CIA), and I was told that I must sever my contact with her.

I was stunned because I had always valued friendships and put a lot of time and effort into developing them. But it was made very clear to me that I had to find a way to back out of the relationship. I started begging off from lunches, and when she telephoned, I had to find excuses about why I could not talk to her. Over a period of a few months, she stopped calling and our friendship languished and died. She never knew why. I had no recourse and could not explain it to her.

After that, whenever I met the wife of a potential target, I put up a wall, and while we became acquaintances, I never allowed myself the luxury of developing a friendship with her. I found out the hard way that it hurt much too much. I have missed my friend and still find myself thinking of her every now and then and wondering how her journey through life has been and what her children have grown up to be and if she is happy. I will never know, and there is a part of my heart that is always saddened by this void.

I think that this is why we women have kept up our friendships with other agency wives. We can speak freely with each other and do not have to be on guard all the time. When you are an agency wife, there is a part of your life that can never be revealed to people on the outside. Even when we write these stories, we all know that there is a large part of our lives that will remain secret. That's just the way it is.

Cover Doesn't Cover

During our first tour in the Far East, my husband was given a unique vehicle for his use. When he went out in the evening, he drove this vehicle to one of the hotels, parked it there, and then took taxis to the safe house where he had agent meetings. Good tradecraft. My neighbor came to me one day and told me that she felt so sorry for me. I asked why and she said it was because she was positive that my husband was having an affair or perhaps more than one because she had seen his vehicle parked at different hotels around town! I could not explain to her why he parked his vehicle at these sites, so I just said that I was certain that once we left this post, he would see the error of his ways and we could rebuild our marriage. I always felt like a traitor to my husband because I could not defend him. I also felt that she must have thought that I was really stupid because I did not get upset over this information.

This was exactly how agency life seemed to me—you knew what it was all about but you could not tell anyone else. My family thought my husband had a difficult time keeping a job because we had four tours in a row, all under different covers. If you looked at an address book under our name, you would think that he job-hopped all over the world. This is very difficult to explain to families who have lived all their lives in one city and worked for only one employer.

Looking for Trouble in All the Wrong Places

The phone rang in the middle of the night. It was our counterpart in the Thai police. "You must come down here immediately," he cried. "Very bad. Very bad." We both got out of bed and dressed in a hurry. What could be wrong? The Lumpini Police Station was not far from our home. We careened through the silent streets in record time and pulled up in front of the dusty steps. There were six police cars out in front. The good colonel was waiting for us. "He is a very bad boy," he lamented. Who? What?

It seems one of our fair-haired case officers had had quite a night on the town. Again. He had a reputation for frequenting the night spots. The bars of Patpong Road were tempting to the least curious of the lot. I had even met a teacher from Euclid, Ohio, in one of them. These girls could perform the most incredible feats with parts of their anatomy. Have you ever seen a dart fired from between a woman's legs burst a balloon? Don't try it in the comfort of your own home if you value your wallpaper. Most of the bargirls were young girls from the provinces who had been "sold" into prostitution for the sole entertainment of men. Sad but true. But most of us just went and watched and then went home.

This guy did not. It seemed he had had a large amount of Singha beer and the bill was exorbitant because he was paying lots of money for all those orange juices that those lovely legs were drinking. Our case officer friend was at the police station, locked in a cell. It seemed that he had gotten into an argument with the tourist police, then got into a taxi and became belligerent with the taxi driver, so the police arrested him. He got into another fight at the police station and they had had it. The police locked him up, and he was going to stay in that putrid cell with no running water and a cement slab for a bed. No way. Yale law-school types had not bargained for this when they made the decision to join up to be a *spook*. He had this horrible look on his face, pleading for help. Sometimes I ponder if a better lesson would not have been learned if we had just left him there for a couple of days. But we did not.

The police colonel who was a friend of ours said he would help us gain our friend's freedom, but we must promise that he would leave the country within twenty-four hours. Since negotiations are the game, we agreed with one small stipulation. My husband whispered in his ear and we soon departed the station with our wrinkled colleague and the page torn out of the police station activity book report for that night. Cover your tracks, they always said.

It was a long ride home that night, but it was an even longer ride home the next day on Pan Am for our party animal. We walked into work the next morning and there was his desk, empty.

I am sure that his wife who stayed behind to pack out did not find this at all amusing.

The Bomb and The Zombie in Saigon

Il etait 10h 35, le 30 mars. 1965. Une camionnette Citroen noire s'arrete devant l'ambassade americane. It was 1035, March 30, 1965. A black Citroen mini-truck arrived at the American Embassy.

Saigon Post

I was to meet my future husband. I was a secretary and he was a case officer at the station in Saigon. We fell in love in the "Pearl of the Orient" and decided to get married there when my tour was up in June 1965. I would have to leave if we married sooner. A lot of things happened to me that year. Cabarets, French restaurants, hawker's egg noodles, the PX. Let the good times roll!

Four of us worked on the mezzanine floor, a big room with large windows facing the narrow side street on the east side of the embassy. We surveyed two lanes of congested traffic, buzzing blue-and-yellow microcabs, groaning ugly two ton trucks, animated cyclobuses hauling Vietnamese shoppers, street hawkers, pedestrians walking in all directions on the deteriorating asphalt surface. Directly across from our office was a perpendicular cross-street. The corner store was occupied by a small open-air restaurant crammed with wooden tables and chairs too small for most embassy personnel. We frequented the nearby Club Nautique, a private but open-to-foreigners boat club just off the Saigon River. Excellent filet of sole, Pastisse. Not the noodles and tea available across the street.

Shortly after arriving in Saigon, I had the good fortune to take an R&R trip to Bangkok. About twenty case officers and five secretaries, I included, showed up at the airport in Saigon. We were told to wait in the restaurant upstairs, as the plane had not arrived yet. This was no real restaurant, and one Biere 33 led to another to another. The morning passed and so did much Biere 33. We were in pretty fine shape when, at last, the Caribou wheeled in. Cheering, we boarded and to my surprise, several coolers of beer were loaded with our bags. One of the secretaries was a pretty red-haired girl. We had chatted a bit during the long wait, and I thought I might have found a friend. She worked on the top floor of the embassy, in the chief of station's office. As she had just arrived in Vietnam, I did not know her. She appeared innocent and freckled. As the pilot surveyed his tipsy cargo, he decided he had room in the cockpit for her. The Caribou airplane had steps above the flat cargo bed with pull-down canvas seats lining the sides, now filled with noisy beer drinkers. To avoid over-flying Cambodia, we headed South from Saigon and entered the Gulf near Rach Gia. Saigon was a beautiful city of wide boulevards, and it looked wonderful from the air.

March 30. We four office-mates were startled by the pop, pop, pop sound coming from just below our office windows. Like lemmings, we raced to the windows to see what the White Mice were doing. The tiny Saigon police wore white uniforms and earned their name from their appearance. They drank tea in the little restaurant across the street, and there were always many of them in sight. We saw two, maybe more, returning fire toward the embassy. I could see part of a small Citroen panel truck directly below us. It must have been half over the curb, half in the street. Whoosh!

Standing in the rubble of red bricks, I found myself entangled in the wood frame that had supported our precious damned windows. I was pinned between this very large and heavy frame and a desk. The room was full of dust. No one said anything. I made my way back to my desk, remembering my sunglasses were in the center drawer. Found them. They were very dark sunglasses. The room was a mess. One by one, the other three left the room. Still no one spoke. I stood behind my desk for several minutes, struck dumb. It then occurred to me we had classified material everywhere. Picking it up was nonsense, but I did manage to lock the four-drawer safes. I zombied into the open hallway, which encircled the open atrium, looked down to the diesel generator installed on the ground floor, and thought how useless it was in this emergency. I looked up and saw a line forming on the first floor (ground, mezzanine, first). I went to a tiny staircase and up a flight, joining the queue. Still, no one spoke. We were in line for a restroom to wash up. As I stood in line, I noticed the chief of station in the same line. I wondered why he was not up four more flights where his office was located. When I washed, I realized my face was a bloody mess. My eyes were full of debris, as was my hair. My dress had cuts in the material. I walked like a zombie to the ground floor and out the front door. Four hours later I was given a butterfly bandage for my elbow. I wandered over to our other offices in the embassy annex, and reported for duty a little after three in the afternoon. The annex, a half block from my office, was unaffected except for the loss of power. I was encouraged to go home, and I drove my own car to the house. A small window broken, but otherwise the car was just dirty.

The next day, I again reported for duty, mainly because I could not stand the boredom of being at the house alone. Needless to say, my newly hired servants were wary and kept to their quarters, fearing fear itself. I was a zombie alone again. As one of the least injured, I did not realize the effects of 200 kilos of C4. I began to realize I had very little memory of events after the blast. Just a few points were clear, those recounted here: one day with but a few minutes of memory.

The third day, I attended the funeral for the red-haired girl. She had taken a piece of shrapnel in the jugular. A medical doctor was seated just a few feet away, but was so numbed by the concussion, that he watched helplessly as her blood shot across the room.

I forget how I got to the Theater at Tan Son Nhut airbase for the funeral of the little red-haired girl. The final toll: Americans, 2 dead, 47 wounded; Vietnamese,

18 dead, 126 wounded; The Viet Cong had struck American territory, our embassy.

I did marry that case officer in June and left Saigon. I left a part of me behind: the innocence of indestructible youth.

I Led Two Lives

There was a large international community in Mogadishu, and our net was widely cast, particularly for operational reasons, toward those who would have better access to Somalis. Lingering Italians who had forged close relationships with Somalis, possibly through three generations who might run a hotel, a restaurant, or a plantation could be good sources. African or Arab embassies or those with commercial purposes sometimes had valuable contacts, as did the Soviets. The Soviets, however, were a different case as any who would be given permission to fraternize with Americans was most likely employed by the KGB or GRU. Nevertheless, there still was much we could learn from them.

The international community was isolated from the rest of the world. Permission to drive beyond twenty-five miles outside the capital necessitated weeks of advance notice, possible denial on the day of departure, and the need of toting all gasoline, water, and food. A designated Somali security person would always "surreptitiously" follow our every movement.

The office opened for business at 7:00 A.M. and closed at 1:30 P.M. For the most part, the real work of befriending and making contacts among those who had "interesting" connections took place in the afternoons and evenings. It was a happy circumstance to be able to spend more time with the children—our afternoons were free to engage them in our activities. Unknown to them, the children's lives were planted in a life of duplicity that we had chosen. The purpose of getting together with "friends" as a family was often not as it appeared. A child's godfather could be an agent; a nice man that we trekked into the bush with to look for wild game with our children could be of operational interest; the "chance" meetings at the Italian beach club (*Circulo d'Italia*) with a walk on the beach might unveil some talk of dissident secretive movements.

Our involvement with the International School that our children attended was not totally for altruistic reasons. My husband became head of the school board. The principal as well as several teachers were married to Somalis. The children were from embassies around the world, from the World Health Organization and other international businesses or aid groups as well as half-Somali offspring of the staff. I did some substitute teaching and was involved with organized extracurricular activities. Meeting parents through the children, especially those with good relations to the Somalis and contacts that could be helpful, was a large motivating factor.

The objective of all leisure was to marry it with opportunity. The ramshackle but accommodating beach cabin that we rented skirted the Indian Ocean, only minutes away by car. Lashed by tumultuous waves on its rocky front appendage at high tide, the back of the cabin was carefully scrutinized by Somali security. Mostly useful for fortifying relationships with other westerners, the outpost was ideal for informal entertaining.

One morning I was alone at the beach cabin preparing for guests who would arrive later when one of my Somali colleagues at the language school saw me and came running over. I was horrified that she would take that chance.

Like many Somali women, she was tall, slim with a graceful elegance, with the kind of dusky fine features that inspire poets and addicted lovers of beauty. A graduate of a prestigious university in the US, she had just returned to Somalia with aspirations of doing something significant for her country when the coup d'etat took place. Her brother, who was highly placed with the former government, was immediately imprisoned, tortured, and put under house arrest (years of solitary confinement came later).

She wanted to talk of her personal situation and of her dreams. I felt the burden of an aching call for peace from another soul. I had no easy answers. We kissed good-bye and, as I watched her from the shadows of the window, two men walked up to her and they went off together.

Later I learned that she had been arrested, tortured, and imprisoned for two months for allegedly plotting a coup. Much later she would risk her life disguised as a man during the secrecy of the night to board one of those pickup trucks jammed with refugees and their paltry possessions to be transported over the border to Kenya. She would later use London as a base of operations to garner dissident support and to meet with heads of state to solicit money and aid in her efforts.

My days were filled with duties, obligations, and the overall organization of our lives along with the meticulous guarding of a hidden life. The haunting human misery that was always just outside the walls of our villa rode the waves of my soul's unanswered musings: To think the earth actually provides all the means for everyone on this planet to live a healthy and happy life. Yet it is not to be, because we earthlings are not of a higher consciousness. Greed and a deep disbelief that we are truly all brothers and sisters keeps us from the possible.

Three Weeks With Oleg

It is amazing what a wife is asked to do for "the good of the agency." It was the seventies and we were just home from overseas, assigned to CIA headquarters in Langley. We occasionally became involved in intelligence operations in the Washington, DC, area and enjoyed the diversion from pushing paper in the bureaucratic hallways of the "big gray building." There was a student exchange program between the US and the Soviet Union. The US sent graduate students in their twenties to Moscow for one year and the Soviets sent graduate students in their forties for one year at various US locations. Most of the American students were language or liberal arts majors, and the Soviet scholars were technical experts.

One such Soviet exchange student was Oleg, a thirty-five-year-old, married radio engineer from Novosibirsk in Godforsaken nowhere, Siberia. He was assigned to do graduate work at the University of Maryland. My husband was a graduate of the U of M and was able to arrange a contact with Oleg, posing as a member of the hospitality committee. A friendship developed. We took him to his first football game at Maryland U, and he proclaimed it a stupid, slow-moving sport. The guy had my vote after that. We entertained him at our home. Our intent was to assess his potential for recruitment during his one short year in the US.

Christmas time arrived and Oleg told my husband that the dormitories would be closed and he would have to move out for three weeks. What a break for the CIA and what a nightmare for me. We graciously offered to let this Siberian sleep in our guest room for the holidays. He quickly accepted and said he would have to get approval from his control person, a known KGB officer.

My husband had introduced himself to Oleg as a real estate salesman, and Oleg appeared to accept his story. There was some concern that when Oleg checked with his KGB contact, we might be named as CIA people. We had previously served overseas working with local security and intelligence services and had, perhaps, been identified as CIA to the Soviets. But evidently we had lived our cover well, or they had an inefficient filing system, and we passed. The agency was delighted as it was an excellent opportunity to get a close, first-hand evaluation of Oleg. I was stuck with this Russian for three weeks over the holidays with my mother visiting and my six-year-old son looking forward to the holidays.

My father's family came from Russia, and it was very easy for me to relate to Oleg. Too easy—he wanted to talk all the time. He had a ten-year-old daughter and missed his family very much. He didn't understand that American women had chores to perform that required untold amounts of energy to reinforce the art of conspicuous consumption on the granddaddy of American holidays.

Oleg loved to read the "Wash Post," as he disparagingly called it. He hated the newspaper because "it printed lies about his country." When I came home from work at the agency, where I was employed as a "staffer," all the lights in the house would be off with the exception of one tiny lamp right over his head. He said we wasted too much energy in our country. I would arrive to find him with articles circled in the newspaper that he wanted to discuss with me. I recall one that spoke about the lack of snow in Russia that year and how it would hinder the spring crops. He suggested that since America was so wealthy and generous, perhaps they could ship some of our snow to Russia. I am proud to say I did not respond.

I decided it was time for a little culture. Mother, my husband, and I had tickets to *Jesus Christ Superstar* at the Ford Theater. My husband kindly offered to let me take Oleg in his place. Oh, the things these men do in the name of sacrifice. Oleg's English was probably not good enough to understand what a character from the

Bible was doing dressed up like Elvis Presley, but I decided to forego explaining it. Besides, the guy was an atheist anyway. I enjoyed it. He did not.

In order to introduce another Russian-speaking CIA case officer into the orchestrated scenario, we took Oleg to a bar/restaurant in McLean. The place was called *O'Toole's*. It was once reviewed by the Washington Post and I am proud to report *O'Toole's* got no stars. It was a spook hangout and the "earth people" would occasionally wander in by mistake, take one look at the memorabilia on the wall, and pronounce it a private club. Where else could you find an actual street sign from Patpong in Bangkok? Or a bloodied Pathet Lao flag from Site 98? Or a life-size photo of an old case officer whose claim to fame was a twenty-two martini lunch on Sukhumvit when he went back to work? Oleg failed to grasp the significance of these hallowed walls.

We introduced our Russian linguist, posing as a state department officer named "Pat". That should have been a warning sign as no State Department Officer is ever named "Pat." But it worked. Pat and Oleg went out together several times. Actually, Oleg kept asking us to take him back to *O'Toole's*. He really liked it.

We tried various techniques in our assessment of Oleg. About halfway through the visit, my husband switched from the Mr. Nice Guy routine to become more aggressive and argumentative with him. The objective was to try to provoke Oleg to open up and become more forthright with his feelings. I became the understanding, sympathetic wife and he complained frequently to me that my husband didn't understand Russian people. Actually, I'd known that. He'd been married to one for years.

It was decided that, for several reasons, Oleg was not a candidate for recruitment at that time. The holidays ended, and Oleg went back to the dorms. He was due to return to the Soviet Union in June. However, he left unexpectedly in May. We got a postcard from him just before he left that said "Thanks a lot. I tried it your way. It didn't work."

The FBI had been monitoring Oleg's activities at the University of Maryland and we learned what had happened.

The head of the engineering department where Oleg was working was retiring. There was a spirited contest between two men to replace him. Oleg actively campaigned for the candidate who lost. The winner did not like the fact that Oleg had become so involved in the internal politics of the department and asked him to leave a month early.

It was a wonderful, tiring, frustrating experience. That is what intelligence is all about. You win some, you lose some, and sometimes you don't know whether you have won or lost. The outcome may be years away on another continent under a different name. Perhaps Oleg is now head of the chamber of commerce in a small town in Montana using another name or a professor in Moscow. We'll never know.

The Big Purse

I never carry a big purse anymore. I'll tell you why. It goes back about thirty years and starts in a small town in Southeast Asia, long before the days when I thought about the size of a purse.

We were stationed in Danang, South Vietnam. There were only two American couples there. Translate that to read two American women in town. There was a large contingent of military in this "police action" before they called it a war. We worked hard and we played hard. Sometimes we combined the two. When the sun went down we gathered to review the day, frequently at our house because it was one of the few comfortable places in town. After all, we had maids, nice furniture, good food, the latest in tape recorders, and the newest tapes. We probably played "The Green Green Grass of Home" ten times a night. And did we ever have booze! Johnny Walker Black label was two dollars a bottle at the PX. We would strategize half the night about how we could win this "crazy little war." Down on our hands and knees drawing pictures of provinces and ports and airfields. From time to time, after the fifth scotch kicked in, the G2 advisor would decide it was time to take a plane up and see if we could get some flack from the enemy. Drunk? Didn't matter, we weren't flying the plane anyway. And so we did it. It would have been some surprise if we had gotten shot down and I had appeared in my Bermuda shorts and sandals, a twenty-four-year-old CIA wife on some lonely mountain pass. Didn't even think about it. We were too young and too idealistic to believe that anything bad could happen to us, although it was happening all around us.

Well, the "police action" became a war and we finally left before it was over, so we didn't have to take a helicopter off the top of the embassy in Saigon. There were other wars to fight and other planes to fly and other scotches to drink. And so we moved to another city in Southeast Asia. Bangkok was sophisticated. We had friends, servants, restaurants, jobs, and that ever-present cheap scotch. We went to after-hours clubs three or four nights a week with other friends from the office. All trying to get the last gasp of life out of each wonderful day.

Our servants were the best; our house boy would dress each evening and appear when we came home from work in starched white shirt and trousers to greet us with his sterling silver tray and shot glass to mix our drinks. Now, when I say cheap scotch, I obviously mean dollar cheap, not brand cheap. We had the best of everything from the big PX in Klong Tuoy. The variety was too vast to imagine: liquor, cordials, wines, beers, cognac, and a few odd selections thrown in, like Fundidor Brandy. I liked Ernest Hemingway, and all his wonderful woe-begone existentialistic characters drank Fundidor. Then there was the Pernod phase. Pernod came into Thailand from Laos, where all the French expatriates drank it. It was the drink of artists and authors and magnificent lovers, and most probably, a lot of drunks in Paris. How nice to sit around on Sunday morning when our friends dropped in to discuss some off-beat topic and get wasted on that wonderful clear liquid that tasted like licorice and became opaque when water was added. I had a long love affair with Pernod one year. I had love affairs with life during those five years. I remember discovering that scotch and soda was the safest thing to drink. We would work all day, come home and say hello to our child, eat a gourmet dinner that the cook had made, and we were off. There was a large contingent of us who ran together (minus the bulls) during those wonderful days. The city was sultry, sexy, and stimulating. It relentlessly assaulted all my senses. The city thrust its seductive arms around me. Sensual indulgence was everywhere. Filipino musicians played the latest tunes from the States almost before they were popular in New York. We had our favorite haunts and when a crowd of us would walk in they would play our favorite tune: "Snoopy," "Leavin' on a Jet Plane," "A Taste of Honey," "Sitting on the Dock of the Bay," and on and on and on. We never drove our cars, preferring taxis or drivers when we had "overindulged." I overindulged in life, and it was glorious. Our servants did not know our friends' names. They were simply known as Master Martini, Madame Rum and Coke, Master Gin and Tonic, and Madame Martini. Madame Martini was actually married to Master Martini and didn't even like gin, but we understood who she was. And so it went—a crystal-clear haze of still-remembered sultry, ice cube-tingling memories that still make my skin tingle and bring a silent smile when I want to steal away for a moment. We went our separate ways to new assignments, to buy houses in the suburbs of northern Virginia, to new locales and new experiences. But we will always have Bangkok. Once in a while when I am pumping gas, shopping at a supermarket, driving down the highways of life or writing this book, I pause a moment, I remember and I smile.

The purse? Well, the war was over and we came in second. Back to the States and a responsible job in China Operations at headquarters in Langley. Working with Chinese, selling real estate, and not having enough hours in the day what with raising a child, caring for a house, working, and socializing in a normal routine. Everything was pretty wonderful. Then it came again. Overseas. Resign the job and try to get a new one there. Only this time it was different. Europe. A nine-bedroom house in the suburbs of Copenhagen, far from the city. No servants. The chief did not believe in "working wives." No opportunity to work on the economy without a work permit, which took a year. Daylight lasted only a few hours on a winter day so close to the Arctic Circle. Had some fun. Took some language lessons. Joined a little theater group. Cleaned the "castle." Waited for my husband to come home from the office. Well, one morning, depressed and pondering the meaning of life, I made myself a vodka and grapefruit juice and said to myself, "This is not good." But it *was* good. Very good. I forgot my problems and boredom and a quiet glow appeared. Well, the tour ended after a year and there were only a few "glow days." You have probably figured out where this was going. I did not.

Back to the States one more time. Into the old house and husband back to work in the old building. Child in the same old school. Mother has a lot of time on her hands. Find a job or have your own cocktail party. What to do? It was easier to have the cocktail party. Only problem was that no one came. Drinking alone was becoming a regular morning ritual. But I could usually pull myself together by the time school was out. Took a "nap" and appeared all ready to start the next round of baseball and soccer games. Oh, yes, I was the mother who drove everyone home. No one ever knew at this point. But something was happening. I was losing my tolerance and, I thought, my mind. But I did not care about life around me. I couldn't get excited about anything. Birthdays, home runs, new babies, happy people, beautiful sunsets...it did not matter. I didn't have a job and no incentive to get one. I would only have to move again.

Just about then the word came from the personnel department in Langley. We (I use that term loosely) had been given an assignment in California. Now surely I could get excited about that. I did. This would be a chance to start over again. New place, new friends, new school, new surroundings, and a new job. What a deal! Farewell to Langley. Farewell to boredom. The only problem was I took myself with me. The chief of my husband's section said that they needed a wife to work in the office out there. Was I interested? You bet I was. I filled out all the paperwork prior to my departure and we set out in our brand-new car with kid, mother, husband, wife and a box on the top that they called the "cockroach." Forgot to mention there were a couple of half gallons packed in the back for our cocktail hour on the road. It was a wonderful trip across the United States. Things were looking up.

We arrived in Los Angeles and found a wonderful house and met our new boss. I went into the office with my husband to meet him. He told my husband that he did not think case officers belonged in the office. They needed to be out on the streets where the action was. His exact words: "I don't want to see you. I don't care if you are out sitting in a bar playing with some girl's tits. Just don't hang around the office. Develop some assets." I must say I cared if he was sitting in a bar playing with some girl's tits. But being the dutiful wife, I laughed and agreed. He was interested in having me come to work—waiting for the paperwork and clearances were the only holdups.

A month after we arrived and were settled in our small mansion in beautiful downtown Pasadena, the chief of the division came out for a visit. Since we had the biggest house at the base, we offered to host a cocktail party for him. It was a gala affair with lots of good booze, food, company, and no agents with tits. The division chief had several martinis and then took my husband aside at the end of the party and told him he had good news and bad news. The good news was that my clearance had come through; the bad news was that he did not believe in wives working for the agency. I would probably have ripped his head from his lower body if I had known this. I ranted; I raved; I wrote a letter to Langley protesting my treatment, and I got drunk. The ranting and raving and the letter to Washington did absolutely no good. Getting drunk did. It was the beginning of a long friendship with running away from life. What to do now? I couldn't type. They didn't have that in my college course requirements. I think they figured if you could think, it was good enough. It wasn't. I took a course at the local community college and learned to type. I got a minimum-wage temp job at the Jet Propulsion Laboratory typing formulas for eccentric scientists who had to be reminded to change their clothes every five days. And I started drinking more. I didn't want my husband to know this, so I bought my own liquor, and when I ran out, I watered his bourbon down and fixed him his "bourbon and water" right out of the bottle. I must admit he sometimes wondered at the color of his Jim Beam, but who cared at that point? Let him wonder. He had a job and an exciting life, and for all I knew, he was reaping the benefits of some girl's tits, too.

Our tour in California was over, and it was back to Langley. Old house, old school, old friends. I was offered a job through an old friend. I jumped at it. Downtown Washington, D.C. location, expense-account luncheons, rushing up to the Hill to cover Senate hearings—just my cup of schnapps. I took it. By now I was "maintenance drinking," which in the "Corps of Alcoholics" means that I was drinking enough to reach a comfort level but not enough to get drunk. I did well in this job. I got some self-esteem back, and earned the respect of my peers and bosses. Since I had to have alcohol to function, I had to have it with me at all times. I carried a big purse. I could step out to the ladies' room, have my own little cocktail party in the farthest stall, and get back to my office with no one the wiser. But something happened. My tolerance was failing. I was starting to forget what I was doing. I often stayed after work at the bars along Connecticut Avenue drinking with coworkers. I drove home drunk. I couldn't handle drinking at lunchtime anymore. I hid bottles in the bedroom closet, in other big purses on the shelf, poured vodka into coffee cups for my morning drive over Key Bridge from McLean. I did not care about my appearance, my bills, my taxes, my child, my mother, my husband, myself. I knew that drinking was the problem, but I could not stop. I lost weight. I did not eat or sleep much. When I woke up in the middle of the night I drank scotch and I brushed my teeth with a vodka and grapefruit chaser. But I still kept dragging myself into the office, and they did not seem to notice. You see, I did not want to be an alcoholic and if I had a job, good address, perfect family, and a briefcase and a sports car, I couldn't be one, could I?

And then something wonderful happened.

It was a day like any other day. December 23, 1982. The office was closing for the Christmas holidays, and we had one last luncheon before we left. I had one drink. It hit me. I couldn't function. I just sat there in a daze. My husband was called and came down to pick me up, and I went home and "fell asleep" on the living room floor. He evidently left for a while and returned with a friend. In his hands was my purse! Slowly, he reached in and pulled out the scotch bottle. "This is not social drinking!" he said. No shit, Jim Beam, even I knew that. The friend he brought with him had just been sent home from one of our stations overseas at the "request" of the agency, short of tour, and tossed into a treatment center for his alcoholism. I never went to see him there. We all knew why he was there. He was doing well and looked better, and I did not want to hear about that. With dread, I listened. They had made a reservation for a bed at the same alcoholism treatment ward! And it had my name on it. No, no, no! The Christmas cookies were not made; we were hosting a New Year's Eve party and everyone would know, I protested. "They already do" were the cries around me. My husband had contacted the medical department of the agency, and they had suggested this treatment. "You are going to die if you don't get help," he said. "Soon?" I asked. And then it happened. I don't know where it came from or how it got on my lips. I knew that tomorrow was not going to be any different than today if I did not stop. I knew that I had an illness and it had nothing to do with where I'd worked or where I lived or how cheap scotch was. I had tried will power, church, a shrink, a priest. Nothing had worked. "I'll go."

That was seventeen years ago, and I have not had a drink since. In my wildest dreams, I could not imagine how my life would change. Same house, same kid, same job, same husband. But not the same me. Hard work and thousands of meetings with other drunks just like me have afforded me the luxury of living one day at a time and I savor every moment. But that's another story for another book.

By the way, I always carry a small purse.

Chapter III

I DON'T THINK WE'RE IN KANSAS, TOTO

"The plumbing is non-existent, the air conditioning doesn't work, and it's difficult to read at night by candlelight. But smiles, serenity, and pure contentment prevail. I ponder such different lifestyles and I wonder who really has the answer to a perfect world! Not I."

Mariellen O'Brien
on her departure from Chiang Mai, Thailand

Heads or Tales

Fresh pork was available in abundance in Ethiopia, and fresh meant that you literally went into the butcher shop to order fresh spare ribs and the butcher gave you a time frame of how long it would take. Then he disappeared for a while and next you would hear loud squealing. The butcher would then appear with your blood-dripping ribs. Most Ethiopians spoke Italian, which they had learned from the Italian occupation troops; and a lot of them could also speak some English. Often, when dealing with merchants, you had to combine English/Italian/Amharic and hope for the best. One time I stopped at the butcher shop to pick up some dog bones for our dog and I asked the butcher for "ossi" (which is close to "bones" in Italian). He gave me a strange look and did the butcher disappearing act. When he came back, he had this huge bundle wrapped in brown paper and tied with string. When I put the bundle in the car, I noticed a putrid smell but just assumed it was the many bones he had given me. When I got home, I gave the bundle to the maid and told her to boil the bones for the dog. She went off and all of a sudden I heard uncontrollable screaming from the kitchen. I raced in and found an entire horse head on the counter! The butcher obviously had misunderstood my "ossi" for horsey and had one old horse head that was still laying around to satisfy Madame's unusual request. The gardener went off somewhere with the head, followed by all the stray dogs in town.

Walk in My Shoes

Early one Saturday, when we first arrived in Taiwan, I decided to take a walk to the local village with my daughters, ages three and one. I wanted to see how the villagers lived, and since it was a short distance from our compound, I decided to let our one-year-old walk instead of taking her in the stroller.

In the village, we strolled past people cooking "yu tiao" in large vats of boiling oil and savored the smell of the crispy fried pastries. We peered in the window of a barber shop where we saw a father instructing the barber on how to cut his son's hair. Women were already out washing clothes in ditches by the side of their huts. Riders were zipping by on their bicycles, ringing their bells to warn us as they hurried to their morning jobs.

Linda and Nancy were enthralled with all the excitement and different scenes. Suddenly, Linda nudged me and said, "Mommy, look at that little girl who has no shoes on!" She was right; the adorable toddler in the ragged little jumper was barefoot.

I stopped. Although I had not yet learned the language, I thought I would try to talk to her. She was alone but did not seem to be afraid. I bent down, smiled, and took her hand. She giggled a little, turned her head in shyness, and looked up the street. It was then that I saw her mother, who was slowly ambling toward her little one. When she came nearer, I stood up, pointed to the little girl's feet, then to my daughter's feet, and then with a question on my face, shook my head. She shook her head also, meaning "No, she has no shoes." I looked at my own children's shoes and felt such a pang of guilt. How could I stand so bold-faced, proud, with shoes amid such need. I knew what I wanted to do, and instead of arguing with myself, I bent down and slipped my one-year-old's little sandals off her feet. Taking the little tot's hand, I pulled her onto my lap and fastened the sandals on her feet. She smiled and looked at her mother, who, although embarrassed, folded her hands together and placed them in front of her face and nodded her thanks. It was enough. I carried Nancy home, and she never said a word about her sandals. It was right with her.

Ladies of the Night

The oldest profession prevails the world over, but the Far East and Europe seem to approach it with a different attitude than we do in America.

In the Far East, I observed "ladies of the evening" standing in doorways waiting for "GI Joes" to approach them. It happened one evening while out for dinner with two other couples, strolling down the street, husbands ahead of us. Our husbands were approached with a "Want a good time, Joe? Me love you long time." The women did not know that we were only five feet behind and could hear everything. Our husbands had to laugh and turn around and remark that they had to ask their wives. We ate in another part of town after that.

Evening entertainment in Europe was a different approach altogether. In Amsterdam, there was a famous street where the "ladies of the night" sat in storefront windows. The customers window shop and buy when they see what they like. It is not unusual to see the "ladies" in skimpy outfits sitting with the curtains open waiting for customers to stroll down the street. When she gets a "sale," the curtains are closed while the shopper unwraps his purchase.

In Rome, Italy's "ladies" were called Campfire Girls. The customer would drive out to the Tor de Quinto where the "girls" would stand on the side of the road. I use the term "girls" even though most of the women were in their late fifties. They would build their campfires along the road for warmth as well as a way to light the way for their customers. Mussolini had ordered all prostitutes out of Rome, so they ended up on the Tor de Quinto because it was outside the city walls. Now I think that they stay there just because it is convenient; it is not unusual to see the local police supplying the wood for the fires even though prostitution is still illegal.

When I first heard about the Campfire Girls, I did not know who or what they were. I remarked to my eight-year-old that she would not have to worry when we got to Rome. They may not have scout troops, but they most certainly had Campfire Girls. Whoops! I soon learned that these were not the ones who sold cookies.

Repairs

We all know how difficult it can be to get things fixed in the United States. Imagine trying to do that overseas with language barriers and 110-volt appliances in a 220-volt land. It can be a nightmare! During our first tour in Bangkok, the automatic transmission in my Oldsmobile started to have problems. It would howl and jerk at the most inopportune moments, and driving in Bangkok was scary enough during the sixties. (Incidentally, it is even worse now.) I complained enough to my husband that he agreed to find an automobile mechanic. After asking around, he located one who supposedly had lots of experience fixing American cars. He took the car and two weeks later, I asked my husband to check on the car because it seemed to be taking much too long. He came home late that afternoon looking very, very pale. I asked him what was wrong and he told me that when he went to check on the car, the mechanic had the transmission totally disassembled and lying in hundreds of pieces all around the car. My husband freaked out and demanded that the mechanic reassemble the transmission and put it back into the car. We would pick it up the next day. The mechanic agreed and, when we went there the next day, the transmission seemed to be back in the car. We were surprised but also pleased because I was tired of taking taxis and samlors (three-wheeled motor bikes with a passenger seat in back). The car's transmission seemed to be perfect, and so we left, a very happy and satisfied pair of customers. After we got home, my husband asked me if I had seen the other Oldsmobile very similar to mine in the shop. I said that I had, and what did that have to do with my car? My husband said that he thought the mechanic had simply taken the transmission out of that car and put it into my car because there was no way that he could have reassembled all those pieces in such a short amount of time. For thirty years, I have often wondered if that was true. All I know is that the transmission in my car no longer gave me any problems, and it ran just fine for the rest of our tour.

* * *

"The dryer went broke and stopped drying clothes," said her servant. My friend's cook assured her that he knew where it could be fixed. She arranged to have it taken to this little shop and, about a week later, it was delivered back to her house. She was so excited because it was during the rainy season and there was a problem getting the clothes dried on a line outside. She did a load of laundry and opened the newly repaired dryer to put the clothes in it. There, carefully hung and spaced apart were several little clothes lines!

A New Kind of Pasta

Life back in the United States after our return from our first overseas assignment was not the same as before. Oh, our friends were still the same, we still went to PTA meetings, did neighborhood watch, returned to the same jobs, and even socialized with the same Saturday night crowd; but we had changed so much. Our lives had been so enriched with new customs, different foods, exotic cities and countries. These experiences had forced us to grow and our lives were forever changed.

I envied my friends and family because they were still contented with their lives and I found that I was bored with what used to give me great contentment. After two years, my husband decided to apply for a second tour overseas.

Much to our surprise, we were assigned to Rome, Italy, and had nine months to prepare for the move. We looked forward to a European tour after having served our first tour in the Far East.

Since English was not commonly used in Italy, it was recommended that both of us take language training. The agency enrolled us in Italian language lessons, three half-days a week for three months. This would be a survival course that would teach us enough Italian to at least order in a restaurant, shop at the market, etc. By the end of the three months, I was more comfortable using my basic Italian than my husband was. This by no means meant that I was fluent, but I did have confidence that I would be able to manage without too much trouble.

When we arrived in Rome and realized how few Italians spoke English, I knew that I would have to use my basic Italian or be completely isolated. The first day was not too difficult because we had an escort who helped us get settled in. We were invited for dinner by my husband's boss, who had mastered the Italian language after three years in Rome, so he ordered for all of us. The next day was the day of reckoning when I realized how little Italian I knew! I was going to meet my husband for lunch. This did not seem to be too difficult because we were living in a hotel only five blocks away, and I would not have to talk to walk the five blocks. So the children and I went on our merry way to meet Sam at the office. Someone had suggested that we eat at the "American Grill," which was across the street from the American Embassy. Off we went, and I was excited to try my skill at ordering our meal.

The restaurant was very nice—nice people, smiling faces, but then most Italians appeared happy. I still do not know why I thought that our waiter would not speak or understand English, but I did. After we were seated and handed our menus, which were in Italian, I told Sam that I would order because I spoke Italian better than he did. I remembered that my Italian teacher had told us that the portions in Italy were usually very generous and that one could order "mezza" (half order). After all these years, I still remember what I ordered. For the children, I ordered a mezza order of pene, a spicy tubular pasta; for Sam and me, I ordered regular orders of pasta. I was so proud of myself—I had ordered in Italian and had even ordered half portions for the children. After I finished ordering, the waiter bent down and whispered in English, "Excuse me, madame, you just ordered a half bowl of penis!" The tubular pasta that I had ordered for the children should have been "penne" (pronounced pen-nay) and not "pene" (pronounced like penny), which means the male genitals in Italian.

I quickly realized that three half days a week for three months was not nearly enough to learn this beautiful language, so I continued with my language lessons. I am happy to report that my life and language skills got much better, and we spent two wonderful years in the beautiful country of Italy.

It Hurt to Laugh

In early 1964, I was told that I had a fibroid tumor the size of a grapefruit that should be promptly removed. Since our medical facility was in the process of a location move, I was given the choice of either going to Clark Air Base in the Philippines or remaining in Saigon to have this procedure done in the beautiful local clinic run by the American- and British-educated former minister of health. I chose the latter, wanting to be close to my family.

My surgery was scheduled for 8:30 P.M. (before cocktail hour, I prayed). As I was lying naked on the gurney, prepped, the door opened and in walked my Vietnamese doctor and an American man, both stylish in business suits. Dr. Dey casually introduced me to my fellow countryman and asked my permission for him to observe the surgery. Realizing that he had already seen all there was to see, I agreed.

The visitor obviously felt as uncomfortable as I did and asked the normal overseas ice breaker, "Where are you from?" It turned out that we were both from the same general area of upstate New York. There was a pregnant silence then, as neither of us wanted to delve into the likely possibility of mutual friends.

Being a foreign national, I guess that I was given VIP status in this medical clinic because a day or two after surgery, my doctor's wife came to visit me, bearing a very special gift. Wives of host country dignitaries are not often found in the kitchen, so the fact that she had prepared a very special delicacy for me was most meaningful.

Americans tend to put too much importance on the appearance of our food, so it was not easy to act delighted with my gift as I looked at the numerous one-inch cubes of wiggly gelatinous gray blobs on the lovely plate.

I found after dinner that even to swallow one morsel of this was impossible. But it was imperative that I dispose of a decent number of these delicacies so as not to offend my hostess. So despite orders not to get out of bed, I slipped into my private bathroom and tried to flush some of the cubes down the toilet. But they would not go down!

So I dropped to my hands and knees trying to retrieve these globs and wrap them in the only thing I had at hand—flimsy toilet tissue, thinking all the time that I would be caught in the act, and how would I ever explain what I was doing! Fortunately, the first person to walk in the door was my husband, who spirited away the soggy package and disposed of the evidence.

But, oh, how it hurt to laugh!

KAREN L. CHIAO AND MARIELLEN B. O'BRIEN

A Cambodian Refugee Camp

At a party in Bangkok, a group of us were listening to the head of the United States Immigration Service tell about a group of Montagnards who had managed to reach the safe haven of Thailand. Approximately 450 Montagnards left Vietnam en masse, and only about 100 survived to reach the safety of Thailand. Along the way, their numbers had been decimated by Vietnamese soldiers, bandits, starvation, and at one point, poisonous berries. Of the hundred, only about six women and very few children survived. It was such a tragedy for these fearless fighters who had fought so bravely beside American soldiers. What made the story particularly poignant was the fact that, unlike other groups, they refused to immigrate to the United States if even one of them was denied permission to enter the United States. They wanted to be processed as a group. They had left Vietnam as a group and would remain a group. This had never been done before, and it was unlikely that it would happen now, without a special act of Congress. We listeners were swept up by the story of these people who were on the edge of extinction but who were still strong enough to live by the mantra "one for all and all for one." In an age of "meism," this simple concept of unity touched a core deep within each of us. We were overwhelmed by the fact that even though they had suffered so much and the United States represented safety, they refused to abandon each other in order to go. The French named them "Montagnards," which meant "mountain people," but they called themselves Dega people. I call them heroes.

We left that evening, determined that we would try to find a way to help. We had such stars in our eyes and were so caught up by their philosophy that we decided to get together to plan a strategy to change the law of immigration. But first, the six of us wanted to meet with the Dega leaders to see if there was anything we could do to immediately help. So we applied for permission to visit the refugee camp, and much to our surprise, it was granted.

On the morning of departure, we met at the embassy. Strangely enough, all of our husbands were there to say good-bye. We could not believe it. I think they thought that we were crazy and did not believe that we were really going to go through with it. I have to admit that I had a little taste of fear gnawing in the pit of my stomach, but I did not sense that the others were frightened so I tried not to let my fear show. Off we went! To anyone who has traveled on a highway in Thailand, they know that the trip itself is an adventure. The road is like a washboard, so your insides are constantly being bounced about. You find yourself pulling your feet up to your chest to make room for your car amongst two cars who are passing each other. We all spent a lot of time using body language and saying prayers to get us safely to Aranya Phra Thet. After a long and dusty ride, we arrived in Aranya late in the afternoon and checked into our hotel, which consisted of a series of rooms around a garden. The rooms were clean, but very sparse—just a cot with the towel as a blanket and a nightstand. The bathrooms were Thai style, so there was no toilet, just a hole in the floor. But as I said, it was clean and we felt that it was part of the trip. After dinner, we walked around the town. We were all excited to be in Aranya—somehow it almost seemed like a town out of the Old West. We headed back to our hotel so that we could read for a while and go to bed early. When I turned on the light in my room, I discovered that it was only a 40-watt bulb hanging from the ceiling. There was no way that I could read in bed, and I had not brought a flashlight with me. I went next door and knocked on my friend's door and discovered that the light was the same in her room. We decided to have a pajama party and rounded up the others. I had some nuts, and she had a bottle of wine. We relaxed and found ourselves telling each other that we were a little scared by all this. We admitted that each of us was very apprehensive about the next day but had been afraid to voice it. We relaxed and then were able to go to our rooms and fall asleep.

We had to be up at 5:00 A.M. because the van would pick us up at 6:30. I showered and dressed and walked to the nearest coffee shop for a cup of strong Thai coffee and a muffin. The others were there when I arrived. We were eager to get started because the trip to the camp would take about three hours due to all the security checkpoints that we would have to go through. As we came closer to the camp, we grew quieter. The area around the camps had been cleared—probably for security reasons. Suddenly, there was the gate to the camp. One more checkpoint and we were waved through. As soon as we drove through the gate, there was a large group of women and children cheering and waving and they held up a sign that read "Welcome to the American Wives." We could not believe it. We all looked at each other in amazement because we were not there in any official capacity. The camp director came to our van and told us that we were invited to be special guests at a dance ceremony and a lunch that had been prepared in our honor by the women of the camp. We tried to explain that we had not come there officially, but then we realized that he either did not understand or chose not to understand and so we were whisked away to a Cambodian dance ceremony. It was all so surreal—here we were sitting on a hot, dusty plain in Thailand watching these beautiful children dancing their traditional Cambodian dances and trying not to look at those children who had lost limbs or bore other terrible wounds.

We were anxious to meet the Dega, but the camp director had other ideas. From the hospital and orphanage, we were brought to one of the huts, where an elaborate lunch had been prepared. The director told us that a lot of the women had put their rations together and had purchased vegetables from the local farmers and had fixed what looked like a feast. Tears came to our eyes when we realized the sacrifice that these women had made to fix this fantastic lunch for us. We felt like impostors. We were there to meet with the Dega and here we were being feted by these gentle Cambodian women. We thanked our hostesses after the lunch and asked them what could we do to help; they told us of their need for books and pencils and papers so that the children could be educated. There were teachers in the camp but no supplies.

Following lunch, we were finally on our way to meet with the Dega people. We were led to the hut of the head man, Irbut, and met him and the other leaders. The men were small in stature, but when we were introduced to them, they looked like they were nine feet tall. We could see the scars of their journey. They had suffered horribly after the North Vietnamese took over because the Montagnards had helped the American military forces fight the North Vietnamese and Viet Cong, and so the hatred for them ran deep. It had taken them about two years before they finally reached the Thai border and safety.

Years later, I still remember how we all stood in awe of these people. That there were so few of them and that they had suffered so much and yet were willing to give up the chance to find safety in America if one of them was denied entry deeply affected us. It was incredible to see this kind of solidarity.

We left the camp late in the afternoon, much to our driver's dismay. He had wanted to leave earlier because of the road conditions. On the way back to Aranya, we were very quiet. The camp had made a deep impression on us—we could not believe the generosity of the women of the Cambodian camp or the courage of the Dega. When we returned to Bangkok, the first thing we did was collect paper, pencils, books, and crayons. We arranged with a missionary who went up to the camp to carry the things in for us. We made several shipments during the next six months to the children of the camp.

We wrote letters and found out that their plight was already known on Capitol Hill. Fortunately for the Dega, there were a number of senators and congressmen who had served in Vietnam with them, and they sponsored a bill to have them admitted to the United States as a group. Before departure, they had been moved to a holding camp just outside of Bangkok. We arranged to see them at the new camp, and when we got up there, I think that we were as excited about their imminent departure as they were. We asked what we could do to help them with their resettlement, and the only thing they asked was that we bring their weaving loom to the States so that their wives could continue with their ancient art of weaving. One of the women of our group was returning to the States, so she put the loom into her household effects. She and her husband delivered it to them in North Carolina where they had been settled. She told us that they were thrilled to see the loom arrive intact. Even though we had no direct impact on their resettlement, we felt that our interest in them gave them some hope that all would work out. It was an experience that I will never forget. I have always been thankful that I was lucky enough to have met these courageous people.

Hardship Post

There was absolutely no entertainment of any sort in Addis Ababa (fondly called Addis). No movies, bowling alleys, softball fields, or good restaurants. Some members of the American community who had served before us attempted to make a four-hole golf course. But between the rocks and the starving cows wandering around, it was not worth the effort. So, we'd drink. One of the big social events of the tour was piling into the "company" Jeep and going out to the dump to wait for the hyenas to surround us! Then we would turn on the spotlights and just watch them snarling and snapping at the Jeep trying to get inside for a nice feast! The chief particularly liked this little escape from the office, and he had the Jeep specially fitted with four huge spotlights on all corners of the vehicle. The smell of the dump was unbelievable—even worse than the city stench—then add in the hyenas who really stink and what do you get? Fun and games in the Third World.

Another fun thing we did to pass the time was torment TDYers (temporary duty) who had the misfortune to have Addis on their itinerary. The auditors really got the business. There were about fifteen people in the office, and we all went to dinner to the one and only real restaurant in town. Actually, it was out of town quite a distance, and we would take the unsuspecting TDYer who had just arrived from a cushy stay in a city like Rome to this restaurant, which was a holdover from the Italian occupation. An old Italian family owned it and catered to the construction people who were building roads; it also doubled as a hotel and whorehouse. The whores were a collection of women from different ethnic cultures and backgrounds. While we ate, they would just sit and stare at the people at our table. Add three or four moth-eaten German shepherd dogs who looked like they would have loved a delicious human leg and you have an idea of the atmosphere of this restaurant. The local beer was St. George and it was very potent! But when there is nothing else, you learn to accept it. After a few St. George beers that would leave the TDYer gagging, the Italian food would finally arrive at the table. It took forever, meaning they were probably in the back killing something for us to eat.

There was always a little surprise in the shape of a black roach in the lasagna or eggplant dish. We had made a deal that whoever got a live roach in his portion of the food would get a free dessert. When one of us found a roach, we dramatically pulled it out and waved it around so that the TDYer would get a good look. One poor fellow actually retched over this little drama and left the next day for Frankfurt on the one flight a week out of Addis. We saw him years later, and he said that that trip made him realize what a hardship post really was.

My husband (hereafter referred to as Dick) and I had become good friends with the man who was the equivalent of the Ethiopian senior security officer and his family. He had many grand social events at his home, and Dick and I were always the guests of honor for some reason. At a dinner in Ethiopia, the guest of honor is always given the task of slicing the first piece of meat off of the cow that had been freshly killed and was hanging from a tree in the backyard. Dick, as the male guest of honor, would be given a small stiletto knife and ushered to the backyard. The first layer of skin had been removed, so there we were looking at the bloody carcass and being told to "slice away." Somehow, Dick could do it—I never could, but he would cut enough for both of us. Lucky me! Thank God for St. George beer! We would all end up with a hunk of raw beef on our plates and then we would go to the buffet table, which was laden with different bowls of something (I never asked what because I was not certain that I really wanted to know). Our host would say "eat, eat, grow big." At our first such dinner, I thought that I would just die if

I had to eat the raw meat, so I ate what I thought was creamed corn, but it wasn't and it tasted horrible. I spit it into my napkin and somehow managed to push most of the food from my plate onto my husband's plate, which displeased him because he had no place to push his food. But I figured that he was the case officer, I was only the wife, and I did not have to eat this for God and country.

I got a real shock when I went to the bathroom. Wealthy Ethiopians have very nice houses, so I was intrigued when I found a clothesline set up in the bathroom with twelve enema bags hanging from it. They were all different colors. My curiosity got the best of me and I asked the hostess about the enema bags. She laughingly replied, "Oh, those are the purge bags, when we eat raw meat we have to have a physic. Please pick a color!" Right. So the old saying "eat good, poop good" must have originated here.

When I first arrived in Addis, I always saw women squatting everywhere and I actually remarked to someone that Addis must have some sort of public transportation system since so many women squatted around the town waiting for buses. After much hysterical laughter, my friend announced that these women were in various stages of going to the bathroom. . .squat, pee, poop, stand up, straighten out the shamma (national dress robe), and move along. I tried not to stare but found it difficult not to—it was something I had never seen before and have not seen since.

It's My Mediterranean Blood

I complained to my husband that I did not want to take the children to the outing at the farm owned by a very senior government official of the host country because I would be asked why my children (adopted in Central America) did not look like me. Knowing that adoption is not an accepted practice in their culture, I was not about to tell them that our daughters were adopted. My husband argued that this was ridiculous—these were educated people and would not pry, but if they did, I could say it was my Mediterranean blood. I am fair-skinned but dark-haired and dark-eyed like all my Italian relatives. We had no sooner sat down with one other American couple when six men joined us. Through conversation we found that they had all been educated in the United States or England and had Ph.D.s or at least Masters degrees. When my daughter, then about eight-years-old, approached to ask me something, one of the men asked if she was my child. I answered "yes," and he asked why I was so fair and she was so "tanned." The corner of my eye caught sight of my husband's jaw as it dropped. I never flinched, however, as I explained that it was due to my Mediterranean blood and how while I burned in the sun, my mother tanned to a golden bronze just like my daughter. For the next twenty minutes, the conversation revolved around the wonder of genetics. Our fellow Americans were amused by the whole scene; my husband was not.

The Frustrated Sink

I thought that my Italian was coming along well, although I occasionally just Italianized English words as my mother had done when I was a child. On one occasion the plumber was coming to fix a leak in my kitchen sink and the spritzer on my faucet that no longer worked. My Italian neighbor stopped by later to see that all had gone well and that I had been able to explain the problem adequately. I told him no problem but that Mario, the plumber, had been in a very good mood, repeating what I had told him several times to his assistant. My neighbor asked me what I had said and turned bright red when I told him. He then explained why Mario had laughed. I had told him that my sink was "masturbating and the 'thing' (spritzer) no longer went pfftt, pfftt!"

Beads, Borders, and Batik

Preparation for a new post overseas brought about many months of planning, especially what clothing to take. Going to the tropics meant cottons, light colors, open weave, and wrinkle free fabrics—anything that could be washed because dry cleaning services generally were either unavailable or very expensive in most cities.

In preparation for our move to the Far East, I shopped for months for just the right clothing. Soon after our arrival, I realized that our "stateside" clothing made us stand out. This was at a time when it was better for Americans to blend in with the international community as much as possible. What we needed were batik fabrics made into dresses, blouses, and skirts. My husband had safari jackets and leisure suits made, and the children needed all-cotton clothing with no zippers, which either rusted in the rainy season or melted when the maids ironed the clothing.

So like everyone else, I hired a sewing lady to come every week to sew clothing that would help us blend in with the community, with lots of cotton outfits for the children. My friend's seamstress, Modesta, was an elderly Filipina, who spoke no English but loved working for Americans. She worked diligently all day copying styles from the Sears and Penny's catalogues, taking only a lunch break of fish heads, rice, and betel nuts. When she first smiled at me, I thought that her gums were bleeding because her teeth were all red. I found out that this was the result of the betel nuts, a mild aphrodisiac chewed in many Asian countries.

Soon our closets were overflowing. I felt special with my new wardrobe, each piece always being ironed just so. I had clothes in every style, color, and fabric, plus the accessories to go with each new outfit. Sandals were the shoes of choice, and they came in many styles, colors, and best of all, were very inexpensive. My sandal collection soon rivaled that of Imelda Marcos's shoe collection.

After a year and a half, I decided that I had more than enough outfits to wear, so I referred my dear sewing lady to some recent arrivals who needed to adapt their wardrobe to a more tropical look.

At the end of our tour of duty, we found ourselves back home with this wonderful summer wardrobe—I even had embroidered handbags to match my colorful outfits! Then reality set in. Each outfit had to be ironed because it was mostly cotton batik fabric and the maids did not come with them. I was the "ironing lady," and soon we reverted to jeans, T-shirts, suits for work. I put our cotton batik clothing away, and eventually the long dresses and the beaded sandals became big hits as Halloween costumes for my children.

I have kept the beautiful embroidered and smocked dresses that my daughter wore in the hopes that someday I will have a granddaughter who will enjoy wearing them for special occasions.

A Guardian Angel in a Foreign Land

Shortly after our arrival in Manila, the most devastating typhoon in recent history, Typhoon Yoling, was bearing down on the city. We were still in a hotel on Roxas Boulevard, and when I got up that morning and listened to the weather report, I told my husband that I thought our daughter should stay home that day. We were quite far from the school, and the wind was already very strong. My husband disagreed and pointed out that our daughter had already missed a lot of school due to the transfer and he felt it was important for her to go. She and I almost got blown down when we exited the hotel to wait for the school bus. I knew at that moment that it was a bad plan and I should have listened to my intuition, but I did not and I put her on that school bus. When I got back upstairs to our rooms, I turned on the television set to watch "Uncle Bob," who was an American from Walla Walla. I tuned into his program just in time to hear him say that this was the worst typhoon in history and to stay inside and cover your windows to prevent being cut by flying debris and glass. I started to panic because I realized that the height of the storm would hit around noon and, if the school administration had started evacuating the school, our daughter would be on the bus at that time. I tried to call the school to ask the staff to just keep our daughter there but could not get through because the telephone lines were down. I called my husband to ask him to use the radio to reach the school, but he was in a staff meeting and could not be disturbed. I really became frightened when I watched a fully loaded cargo ship being pushed across Manila Bay into the seawall. It was as if there were a giant hand pushing the ship from behind. I thought that if a ship like that could be blown by the wind, what chance would a school bus or my ten-year-old daughter have in that storm? I spent the rest of the morning and early afternoon in an absolute state of panic. I felt so helpless—my child was in grave danger and I could do nothing. I did not even know where she was or if she was alive. Even now, many years later, I still can remember how I felt that day. Parents are supposed to protect their children, and I had sent my daughter out into that terrible storm.

My husband came back around 2 P.M. He asked where our daughter was and I told him that I had no idea. I could see that he was very worried and I asked him why, what did he know that I should know. He told me that the school staff had sent word at 9:30 A.M. that they were sending the children home! When I heard that, I just fell apart. Why, oh why, had I not listened to my inner voice and kept her home? I lay in bed and listened to the wind howl and the rain pelting the windows. My every thought was consumed with the knowledge that my little princess was out there somewhere and how frightened she must be. The wind was so strong that we had sea water driven into our room under the sliding doors, and we were on the 11th floor! We had no electricity, phone, or water, but at least we were safe. Where was our daughter and was she still alive?

By 6 P.M., I feared that the worst had happened. Our daughter would have been home by now if she were still alive. The bus must have been crushed by some debris. Roofs were ripped off and flying like steel missiles through the air. We turned on the battery-operated radio and learned that there had been mass destruction and many deaths were reported. How scared she must be if by some miracle she was still alive. There was no way for us to call anyone.

The storm started winding down around 8 P.M., but when we looked out the windows of our hotel room, there was nothing except absolute blackness. The electricity was out in the entire city. Suddenly, at about 10 P.M., there was a knock on our door and we opened it, hoping against hope...it was a man from the office who came with the message that our daughter was alive and safe at a coworker's house. He had received the message via short wave radio and had come to deliver the news as soon as he could. Even now, almost thirty years later, I remember how I could not stop shaking and how grateful I was to this man who had risked his life to get through to us. I think that I never thanked him enough for what he did. So here is my thank you. You will always be a hero to me.

Needless to say, the next morning we were up early and we found a taxi driver who was willing to take us to pick up our daughter. When I was able to hold her again, I could not let go of her. She told us that the day before, when the bus could go no further, the driver told her to get out and walk the rest of the way. She got out of the bus because she did not know what else to do and somehow managed to walk down de los Santos Avenue to Magallanes Village. We had gone to dinner at a colleague's house a few nights earlier, and somehow, miraculously, she had been able to find their home in the village. My friend told me that she had arrived there about 3:30 P.M. Somehow an angel must have been riding on her shoulder directing her to their house—there is no other explanation.

Driving Woes

Driving in Bangkok in the late sixties was part Wild West and part demolition derby. One had to dodge teak-laden trucks with drivers who always sat side saddle, samlor (three-wheeled motorbikes with a bench seat for passengers) drivers who thought that they were driving trucks, taxi drivers who believed that the shortest route between two points was over the sidewalks, and other cars, plus the dreaded motorcycles. Imagine a city of three million people with approximately ten major roads and you have an idea of the chaos that reigned.

One afternoon at around three, I was driving down Sukhumvit Road, which was a main artery. There was a railroad crossing and, sure enough, I had to stop for a freight train. It was a very long train and drivers started losing their patience. Eventually, cars from behind began pulling into the oncoming traffic lane so that they could get a jump on the rest of us when the train passed. We waited and waited and finally the gates were lifted. There were six lanes of cars facing each other! Gridlock at its finest. It took fifteen minutes to clear the road, and we had to use sidewalks as roadways to do so.

Another day I was on Rama IV behind a large truck. The truck was lurching and swaying and moving very slowly. Suddenly, the wooden sides of the truck fell off and the axles broke. The driver got out of the truck, looked at the broken axles, scratched his head, and just walked away. Apparently, it was not his problem, but ours because we were trapped behind the broken truck.

The winner of all traffic jam stories was the one I just recently read about in Bangkok, where it now takes forty-five minutes to go one block! There is a circle that I call the "circle from hell" at the intersection of Rajdamri, Silom, and Rama IV—major arteries meeting by the Dusithani Hotel and Lumpini Park. I waited for an hour on some days to get through that circle. There are traffic police who regulate the lights. Carbon monoxide, mixed with the tropical heat and angry tempers and horns beeping and motors revving, assault one's senses with a cacophony of sounds and smells. And then one day last summer it happened. The traffic policeman on duty at rush hour simply put all the lights on green and walked off the job. It was well into the night before anyone got to his destination. And it was that traffic cop's fifteen minutes of fame!

The Big One

We were in Manila a very short time when Typhoon Yoling came roaring through. No one had even mentioned the word typhoon, so I was clueless. That morning I awoke to heavy wind and rain outside, shutters banging, and no power. I went downstairs to see what was up and found the maids cowering in the kitchen with the baby, crossing themselves, murmuring "Hail Marys." I still did not get it. They began to cry about a killer typhoon. I decided to make myself useful. The first order of business was to get all the beer out of the refrigerator and into the ice chest with the remaining ice. What else could one do? We scurried around trying to find candles. One maid went upstairs for some reason, and when I went to find out what she was doing, she was in danger of being sucked out of the hole left by the french doors, which had blown out. I was able to grab her from behind by the apron and attempt to haul her back inside. As I did this, the shutters swung back in on my hand, breaking it. In five minutes, my hand looked like a football. I still did not comprehend the seriousness of the situation, so I tied myself to the upstairs balcony and began to scream for help, but the words kept being blown back into my mouth. Then I became a believer! Rooftops, parts of houses, furniture, drapes, and various other items were flying through the air and there was no help in sight. At last the maid and the gardener realized that I had not come back downstairs and came to help me. About eight hours later, personnel from the embassy were able to get into the village where we lived to assess the damage and find out if anyone was hurt. Hurt, yes! But feeling no pain. I just drank all the beer that I had had the foresight to chill.

We were without electricity and water for twenty-two days. We lived by candlelight and drank water that the military brought from Clark Air Force Base. It was a long time before we had another candlelight dinner. We lived through several typhoons after "the big one" and each one got a little easier. Once my friend called me at the onset of a typhoon and said, "Are you ready?" She picked me up in her trusty Oldsmobile Cutlass that could navigate oceans, and we drove to Subic Bay Naval Base to play bingo while the typhoon raged in Manila. We were in big trouble when the office finally located us!

Island Fever

One of the drawbacks of living in Hong Kong was the size of the place, which limited the number of places to go on weekends. We were confined to a space of about twenty miles in any given direction, and on the island it was less than that. We all looked to the sea for some space to roam. Most of us were young and could not afford our own boats, so we had to rely on the generosity of others who did have them. Our chief had a boat and he tried to include us as often as possible, but we still longed to be able to take off on our own.

One day it was announced that the recreation committee (I had not been aware that we had one) had the opportunity to buy a repossessed boat. We were all thrilled because for a nominal sum, we could rent the boat for an afternoon. The recreation committee became the proud owner of the *Wahini*.

My friend and I immediately contacted the reservations officer to find out how many people the boat could hold. We were told that thirty people would be comfortable on the *Wahini*. This was even better than we had expected so we reserved a date and invited twenty-four guests to a cocktail party cruise. We scheduled the party for a little before sunset so that we could watch the sun set off Lantao Island. We worked for a week preparing all the food and buying the liquor and were so excited!

The afternoon of the sailing was rainy, but in Hong Kong (I should say Asia), rain never stopped us from doing anything unless it rode in on a typhoon. Our husbands lugged all the food, liquor, glasses, and napkins to our cars and we proceeded down to the Queen's Pier, where the boat would pick us up. We assembled and waited and waited. Soon we had twenty-eight people who were hungry and thirsty but no boat. It was growing dark and still no *Wahini.* At first we thought that perhaps there had been a communications glitch and that we were supposed to board in Stanley, where the marina was. Finally one of our officers who spoke Cantonese called the marina and was patched through to the boat boy. The boat boy told the officer that the sea was too rough and he refused to leave the mooring. Nothing we said could convince him otherwise, and our cocktail party cruise was grounded. Fortunately one of the couples lived nearby and we moved the party to their apartment.

A week later, my friend and I arranged to take the boat to one of the smaller islands for the day. It was a grand day, and this time we decided that we would board in Stanley. We arrived there and looked for a large boat—after all, it was supposed to hold thirty people comfortably. The only boat with the American flag flying was a very small boat. I said to my friend, "That could *not* be it," and she agreed. However, all the other boats were flying the British Union Jack. We inquired and found out that indeed, that was the *Wahini*. Thirty people, yeah right! Maybe if none of the thirty was older than six.

We had a good laugh and proceeded on our cruise to a lovely secluded beach on one of the smaller islands. Somehow it did not matter that the boat was small because we had a marvelous time and it gave us a wonderful opportunity to spend the day with our children and husbands, swimming and snorkeling. Through the years we have laughed many times about how lucky we were that the *Wahini* did not sail that first day. We had so much food and liquor that the weight of that alone would have sunk the boat—to say nothing of thirty adults.

Passports, Please

Several of us wives attended the Girl Scout Jamboree for leaders, which was held in Garmisch, Germany. We took the seven-hour train ride from Rome on a train filled with Italians of all sorts lugging cases of garlic, fresh fruits, and live chickens. We stopped in a remote little station in the German countryside, where we spied a vendor selling food. We were starving so we jumped off the train to buy some. Before we finished buying the food, the train whistle shrilled, the conductor yelled "all aboard" in German, and we ran back to the train. There was a big German policeman checking passports before we were allowed to reboard the train. We had left our passports on the train. The train began slowly pulling out of the station. We yelled to our friends, who realized our predicament and threw our passports out the window to us. We quickly flashed them to the cop and literally clung to the side of the train trying to pull ourselves up onto the steps. We did get on and fell into a heap laughing when we realized how close we had come to missing the train and not having our passports with us! Worst of all, we were still hungry and had no food, but we would try again at the next stop. We had learned our lesson—always carry your passport with you.

Say What You Mean or Mean What You Say

It's not all fun and games for the embassy officers either. One day my husband called the motor pool for a car to go to the Foreign Ministry. He went down and waited but no car. He went back up to his office and called the motor pool again. He was told that the car with keys had been left out in front of the embassy. "No, no, I need a driver to take me to the Foreign Ministry," my husband replied. A few minutes later, a driver appeared in my husband's office. When they got out front again, my husband asked where the car was. The bewildered driver said, "Oh, you wanted a car *and* a driver!"

I Remember Her Well

After five years in Rome, I felt that I had become more of an Italian than when my parents had taken me from Italy to the United States as an infant. My theory of acculturation was shot though when my son, going to pay the green grocer I had been buying from for five years, found out that I was listed in his accounts as *la straniera*—the stranger!

Who is the Blind One?

My husband proudly explained how he had come to handle the beggar issue in Addis Ababa. He had chosen a blind boy and his guide as the daily recipient of his contributions and ignored all the others. However, the head of the Consular section lived on the corner where these two stood daily and, much to my husband's chagrin, asked what "kind of spook" was he that he had not yet noticed that the two took turns being the blind one!

Oh, Thank You

As we approached the immigration checkpoint, my husband reminded the children not to leave the doors open even for a second when we got out of the car, or the baboons would get in. What ten-year-old listens, right? My daughter jumped out to look at the baboons on the roof of the building and left the car door open. Immediately a giant baboon jumped into the back seat. I tried to shoo him out, whereupon he stole the children's game and hightailed it across the road. He opened the box and proceeded to try to eat the playing pieces. A "colonial" walked over and chased the baboon away, picked up the game pieces and the box, and returned them to me. "Oh, thank you," I said as I thought: "Oh sure, I am going to let my kids play with something a baboon had just been sucking on!"

Cops and Robbers

Every day of our lives in Somalia in the seventies during the revolution revealed a part of a chapter or a footnote to the larger tale of what our being there was really all about. Large, gaudy illustrated billboards all over the capital instructed the population on how they should think. Typical was one showing a large figure with a cowboy hat ("the imperialist") sucking blood from the Somali people. Americans were supposed to be seen as the enemy to Somalis.

One day, while driving alone on a street at sundown, I was stopped by Somali police. They were not clear why they had stopped me and it seemed to be simply a matter of harassing an American. Condescending and in a highly officious manner, they barked out words indicating that my papers were not in order and that I would have to be brought to the police station. Now I ask you, how could a spy's wife not have her papers in order? So off I went to the police station, since no amount of cajoling or proclaiming my diplomatic immunity would satisfy them. Questioning continued at the station while I persisted in my appeal for a telephone call. Finally able to make a call, I got through to my husband, and he and the consulate officer came quickly and, in a very solemn and businesslike manner, demanded my release. The police reluctantly agreed, and I left, still not knowing why I had been treated like a criminal. Harassment was continuous.

Due to the British influence in the northern part of Somalia, driving on the left hand-side of the road was the law. One day it was changed and all cars, donkey carts, motor scooters, and bicycles had to switch to the right. If it had not been for a small volume of traffic and paucity of roadways, the "Keystone Cops" routine would not have been so humorous. At one point I met an acquaintance head on as we each in our own way negotiated a rotary (traffic circle). We stopped, laughed about it and with a casual wave, went on. The donkey carts were the least amenable to change, and head-on confrontations were an everyday occurrence.

None of the vehicles we used had air conditioning, so we always drove with the windows open unless the billows of sand were enough to choke us. I was driving a four-wheel-drive all-terrain truck with my pocketbook next to me. As my husband was away on "temporary duty" (TDY), I happened to be carrying the servants' salaries. Like an unsuspected tropical cyclone, an arm reached in and grabbed the purse, and a young man sped away with the kind of speed rarely seen in such a hot climate! I jumped out of the vehicle and ran after him while yelling "Get him, get him!" In a torrid flash I was running beside giggling Somali women and a posse of young men all sprinting after the culprit. One swift young man sprang ahead of the pack and retrieved my pocketbook and returned it to me. I was very grateful and thanked everyone and offered some money to the young Somali named Ali who had won the race. He flatly refused to take any reward. Weeks later, when I returned to that same area, I was stopped by Ali, who handed me a letter he had had written by a hired scribe. It said in stilted English that he would be happy to receive his just rewards if it pleased me. He could not have accepted my previous offer because it would have been taken away from him by the crowd. It pleased me to reward him.

Cell Block C

Everyone assumes that we live in the lap of luxury—large houses, servants, etc. However, sometimes government-leased premises are far from adequate, let alone luxurious. After twenty-three years with the agency, we were assigned to Jiddah, a post with government-built-and-owned housing. While the units had every modern convenience, such as dishwashers and disposals, they were quite small and lacked space for entertaining more than six people at one time. One admin counselor had come up with the brilliant idea of placing all the families with children in one walled section. He nicknamed it Sesame Street; I called it "Cell Block C." Cell Block C had eight townhouse units housing sixteen adults and twenty children. The only play area was a concrete area directly in front of my door. Needless to say, the noise level was deafening. Our dogs barked constantly as the little darlings tapped on the window to torment them. The front door was the goal post and the area was constantly strewn with bikes, skate boards, socks, shoes, helmets, balls, and trash. I had lived in cities that were considered hell holes, only to wind up living in a place that was worse than a trailer park. Luckily the new admin officer was walking his dog one night and heard the normal racket coming from a pre-bedtime "prison riot." He did everything in his power to reallocate housing as transfers occurred, a move that saved my sanity and the lives of certain urchins, pets, and fellow parental inmates of Cell Block C.

Keep Your Pecker Up

Yet another school for the children and another teaching job for me. Every time we moved, we started over—new kids and new teacher on the block. I was hired to teach first grade, a grade that I had never taught before. The other first-grade teacher was British and she had been at the school for many years. Every time I passed her room after school, she would give me encouragement by telling me "Keep your pecker up!" After the fifth time of hearing this, my curiosity got the better of me and I had to ask her, "Do I have one?" as surely she and I had a different part of the anatomy in mind. She explained that it was a chin, and I explained that to me it wasn't! We had a good laugh over the differences between the Queen's English and American English. We decided that we needed an English/American dictionary and promised to take the differences with a grain of salt and a chuckle!

Who Is the Nonconformist?

My neighbor in Riyadh, never a conformist, ventured out to Euromarche wearing knee-length shorts. Upon meeting a mutawah (religious police) in the store, the mutawah, dressed in a long gown, demanded to know why he, a man, was wearing shorts, to which my neighbor retorted, "And why are you wearing a dress?" The mutawah was too stunned to do anything but laugh as my neighbor made a quick getaway.

The Best-Laid Plans

As agency wives, you live and plan your life in two- or three-year increments. You choose when to have the second or third child depending on home leave schedules, availability of medical assistance, and adequacy of local emergency medical facilities, but even the best-laid plans can go awry. Relatives will say "Well, how could they even consider conceiving a child *there*!" They think that we are dunderheads who fly by the seats of our pants rather than rational couples who plan, outline, and rethink every eventuality, down to coups and evacuations; but after careful planning, who was to know that the government would nationalize the local hospitals, prohibit the well-trained foreign doctors from practicing, and turn back local medical care fifty years just a month after a positive pregnancy test? Who would have guessed that the state department regional medical officer would not be replaced for six months? Who could predict that at twenty weeks you would suffer a miscarriage?

Being away from family during crisis is difficult and you count on your overseas family for support, both physically and emotionally. Luckily for me, the state department nurse was a true professional. The US military doctor did his best to perform a D&C without the necessary equipment. When my resting heart rate later hit 120 and my fever shot up to 102 degrees, he slept sitting up at our house to monitor the intravenous drip that he had hung from the nail that had held the crucifix above my bed. The doctor and the nurse feared that a septic infection had set in, so they made arrangements to medevac me on the first commercial flight three days after the miscarriage. The state department nurse made the travel arrangements for me to be flown to Germany for medical treatment. She reserved two first-class seats for me and one for the accompanying nurse. The seats for me would be made into a bed for the trip. The admin counselor denied the first-class reservation, but my Florence Nightingale countered by quoting the regulation to him and informed him that it could be done as prescribed because she had written the regulation years before. It was very fortunate for me that she was at this post.

It was also fortunate for me that a military spouse was an ob/gyn nurse, and she accompanied me to administer injections of antibiotics and a drug to control the bleeding during the flight. When we landed in Athens, the Lufthansa station manager tried to take my extra seat away, but the nurse protested this and told him that the plane would not leave the runway until both the pilot and Lufthansa had signed forms stating that they would be liable for any problem that ensued as a result of their taking the extra seat away. Needless to say, I kept my seat. I was met by a military ambulance and taken to the then 97th Frankfurt General, an Army facility. There I was mistakenly taken to labor and delivery—nothing like adding insult to injury! I eventually made it into the GYN surgical unit where, just a couple of hours later, I began to hemorrhage profusely. I have never forgotten the sound of the alarm bells or the frantic racing around as they claimed an already occupied operating room for emergency surgery. I awoke in recovery next to a young soldier who kept complaining that his throat hurt. Poor guy, the nurse had to tell him that unfortunately his tonsils had not yet been removed, "so forget about the sore throat—your surgery has been rescheduled!" They had wheeled him out of the OR to make the operating room available for me. The next morning I awoke to find the surgeon seated at the foot of my bed. He said that he was glad to see that although I was white as a sheet, I was going to be okay. He had feared that he would lose me during surgery because I had been losing blood faster than they were able to pump blood into me.

Here I was in Frankfurt, far from my husband and my little son, who were in Addis Ababa. I was scared and in mourning for my lost baby and had no one to talk with and share all this. It was a terrible time for me. I was torn between my medical condition and worrying about my little son, who was five thousand miles away. Was he okay? Did he understand why I was not there? When could I go home? Fortunately, the spouse of the deputy chief was passing through Frankfurt on her way back after R&R (rest and recuperation). She was my angel of mercy. She took me out for a day while I was recuperating. She was the shoulder that I cried on after ten days alone in the hospital. Her compassion meant so much to me.

Years later I was asked if I had ever been in an ambulance as a patient. I said yes but could not remember when—I guess I had attempted to block out the memory, but, of course, certain parts would never leave my mind. Those who think we lead the "perfect" life with servants and nannies don't realize what it is like to experience an illness or death or some other crisis or tragedy so far away from home, country, and family. It is not all fun and games.

We have all been on the plane, in that ambulance, alone at some point, for some reason, scared, worried but determined to survive.

A Life of Contrasts

Before arriving in Somalia I had learned the protocol necessary for a foreign service wife arriving at a new post. I left calling cards for the wives of the ambassador, deputy chief of mission, and director of the United States Information Service (USIS), after which they called me for a private meeting at tea. It was a welcome and informative tradition. My husband and I were then invited by the DCM and his charming wife as guests of honor at a luncheon with American embassy diplomats and their wives. Their spacious contemporary villa, covered with beautiful crimson bougainvillea vines, had a commanding view of the ocean as the waves pounded the shoreline. We sat down to a formal, gracefully sophisticated luncheon with high cuisine served on silver platters offered by white uniformed and cotton-gloved servants. Fingerbowls with a single floating flower, sorbet between courses, and uplifting genteel conversations followed. The novelty of all this failed to displace the reality check of a scene viewed from the car window enroute to the luncheon: a thin and ragged Somali mother squatting on the dirt sidewalk with her two children, one an infant. They appeared to be lying underneath one of those ubiquitous billboards attacking the imperialists. That woman's situation seemed pervasive. The irony of it all was thought-provoking.

But we had our roles to play. We had the rationalization we needed to get through this confrontation with such overwhelming poverty. Still, our guilt was heavy. To help some was no consolation, and any conscious involvement with groups that could possibly help would be to invite anti-American sentiment, suspicions that we were plotting a coup, and possibly being expelled from the country as *persona non grata*.

When I arrived in Somalia, I was in my early twenties and still weathering culture shock, which included acclimatizing to unfamiliar smells. Mogadishu was permeated with the deeply pungent scents of frankincense and myrrh acting as reality veils, of incense to meet every occasion from hair washing to heralding a new baby. At the other end of the smell spectrum were the animal odors or the redolence of the unwashed that inhabited the sweltering, sizzling hot streets or the more subtle but sickening vapors that exuded from the freshly killed meat from the market. My senses had been challenged and by broadening them I would never be the same. One had to acclimate.

Chapter IV

MASTER AND MADAME

Servants were plentiful in developing countries. Salaries were high and the desire to learn English encouraged individuals to work for foreign diplomats. It had its hazards. A young couple from a middle-class upbringing in America might encounter some problems being addressed as "Master" and "Madame." But no one could get along without them. There were no supermarkets, dry cleaners, washing machines or dryers, no baby-sitters to call, no caterers, or shopping malls. It was learning a new skill to have servants. Some of us invited them to dine at our table, only to find them insulted by the offer. Some of them had ulterior motives. We demanded too much or not enough. We struggled with the concept of having servants at all. But gradually, most of us learned to love them.

Life in Mogadishu

I had a cook, house boy, a day guard/gardener, and a night guard in Mogadishu, Somalia. My life, however, was very busy. Constant home entertaining was the life blood, the only form of entertainment and one of the purposes of our being there. Of course, we were forbidden to entertain any Somalis. This might lead to interrogation, torture, and time in prison for them. We would not break that rule.

Our cook, Ahmed, a portly and ebony-skinned man with little round ringlets of hair, was always ready with a smile. He was a wonderful baker, and we all have delicious memories of his mango pie, his dark rich chocolate creation served hot, which was both pudding and cake, and his magic with breads. About twice a year he would go home to the north, Hargeisa, formerly British Somaliland, where his wife and two sons lived with her family. Ahmed liked to read *Newsweek*, which I left around but would not presume to give him as it could become a security issue. I gave him a novel that I had finished, written in English by the only contemporary Somali novelist at that time. When he finished reading it, I asked what he thought of it and he said glumly, "it's just that man's experience." After we shared that book, I secretly wondered if Ahmed could relate with one of the characters in the book who, in his resentment toward the "memsab," the white lady, would spit in her glass of water before serving it to her.

Ahmed also joyfully taught our son some extraordinarily unsavory profanities in Somali. The three-year-old curly haired cherub impishly waited to use his new-found language in front of a group of Somali drivers and guards as he and I were about to enter the American Embassy. To his delight and my bafflement, he received uproarious recognition with laughter. With an embarrassed look, one of the guards took me aside to explain the incident, which I am sure was passed on with embellishments all over town.

Ahmed cooked everything from scratch. Creativity with what was available locally often brought us to the point of substituting most of the ingredients in a recipe. Somehow we made candy, ice cream, chili powder, corn tacos, eggroll skins, and pasta under these conditions. But the one thing we could not get was unsmoked fresh milk. Somali milk was always smoked, and our children hated it. We eventually found one family who agreed not to smoke some of their milk for us. Their little daughter would come to our back steps at five o'clock in the morning with two of my juice bottles full of the warm milk that I would then boil.

We were not allowed to import anything. However, later in the tour we decided to test the waters and sent a small order to Trieste, Italy, for cans of foodstuffs, chocolate and eight kilos of Reggiano Parmigiano. To our amazement, about three months later, amongst the other ordered items, a full wheel of the cheese (about eighty kilos) arrived covered with black worms. We notified the company in Trieste of their error; they apologized that they should have refrigerated the cheese and we should keep it at no extra charge. After Hussein, the gardener, hosed down the monster cheese and scrubbed the worms away, our house became a bustling and popular stop once word spread to our Italian friends that we would share this wheel of cheese with them.

It was like taking the weight of the world upon my shoulders to do the necessary errands. Tattered hungry boys would run in herds after my car when they thought I was going to slow down and park, all the while yelling in English, "Me watch, me watch." It was then up to me to select one boy to watch my car while I shopped. When I returned, the pitiful street urchin would be draped over the car, and perk up to make a show of cleaning the windshield with his dirty rag. I would hand him some change and thank him before continuing on to other errands and "Me-watch boys" or returning to my air-conditioned home behind the ten-foot whitewashed walls.

Buying vegetables in Mogadishu was like being cast in a role in a play where everyone conspired on the script. I'd scrutinize the vegetable or fruit at hand and, looking rather disappointed, ask how much they were. The reply would come in an off-handed way with a flourish of his hand as if they were giving them away. Then I would have to look amused at the audacity that one would think of requesting such an inflated price. I'd then reply with a conceding offer of approximately half of his offer knowing the duplicity of the scenarios. Then he would look around as if he wouldn't want anyone else to witness his selling the produce so cheap. In a resigned-to-this-badgering-woman look he would expertly pack up the tomatoes in an old Italian newspaper in the shape of a cone. I'd politely wish him well and be thankful that one vegetable had been purchased successfully before I went on to the next item to play my appointed role again.

With the heat and humidity, the onslaught of beggars at every turn, cripples crawling around with wooden kneepads, and desperate mothers making gestures with cupped hands toward their mouths, it was shopping in Hell. Knowing that I could not escape all this even if I left the market, I was obliged to play the game.

A Picture Is Definitely Worth A Few Words

Our cook in Danang was definitely temperamental. He had his way and that was the correct way. He had worked for the French before he joined us and felt he needed no introduction to American recipes or products. He touted his command of the English language. Since I did not want to intrude into his territory and since good servants were difficult to find in Vietnam, I gave him free rein in the kitchen on most occasions. But one particular evening was special. The chief of station was coming up from Saigon, it was my husband's birthday, and I wanted it to be elegant. I explained to Thi that we were having special visitors and I would appreciate if he would set the table for sixteen, find some beautiful flowers at the market, and make sure the crystal, china and silver (all purchased from the PX in Saigon, mind you) were sparkling. I also requested that he make a cake for Master's birthday. I showed him the package of cake mix that I had purchased on one of my runs to Saigon. "Oui, oui, Madame. Not to worry." So off I went to work.

We returned home early to check on things and get ready for our guests. I went in to inspect the dining room. It looked beautiful except...in the middle of the table as a centerpiece was a green banana tree branch. I smiled to myself. He'd followed my instructions: "Please put a leaf in the table."

Well, the leaf was quietly removed and the servants had a giggle over that one. But it's not over yet. Dinner went smoothly and everyone had a pleasant evening. It was now time for dessert. "Happy Birthday" was sung as the servants brought in the cake and put it in front of my husband. He couldn't stop laughing. On top of the white frosting, written in bright red letters, it said "Happy Birthday from Betty Crocker," a direct copy of the picture on the cake box!

X-Rated Help

I was six months pregnant with our first child when we arrived in Saigon and my husband was assigned upcountry. Despite this, our life was good and interesting. We lived in a clean row house with American neighbors on both sides two deep. My husband flew into Saigon late Friday evening and flew back out early on Monday morning. We crammed in a lot of living and fun on the weekends. On Friday mornings, I usually went to the PX and stocked up with food and beer for the weekend. We would then get together with friends or go out to one of the excellent Saigon restaurants. This was before the war and all its horror.

One weekend my husband came home and, oh-oh, there were only a couple of cans of beer left in the fridge. I told him that I had gone to the PX earlier in the week and had stocked up. My husband suggested that my neighbor's wife, and one of my dearest friends to this day, had come over and drunk up the beer. No big crisis; my husband went out the next morning and bought another case at the PX—the local beer was not only unfit to drink but contained a formaldehyde-like agent to age it.

Several weeks later, my husband left for Tan Son Nhut Airport before dawn one Monday morning. Arriving at the airport, he was told that his "air machine" had a serious problem and would not be ready to fly for twenty-four hours. No other planes were available, so he came back into Saigon to spend an extra day with me. I was asleep upstairs in our bedroom in the rear of the house. My husband arrived at daybreak to find a very agitated night guard who began making noises and running back and forth to the servant's entrance as soon as he saw him. My husband told the guard to stop and let him in. As the gate opened, an ARVN (Vietnamese Army) major in full uniform ran out buckling his belt. My husband grabbed the guard and asked him what this was all about. The guard, terrified, said he would be a dead man if he told. My husband responded that he might be in the same situation if he did not talk and pulled out his Swedish-K machine-pistol to emphasize the message. At this point, our maid, a very attractive woman in her late thirties, came out sobbing, said she was leaving and would not ask for a reference. As it turned out, while my husband was upcountry and I was sleeping the sleep of the just, our servant was entertaining ARVN officers, drinking our beer, and eating our food. What really bothered me was that this woman had worked for an American MACV (Military Assistance Command Vietnam) colonel for several years and had come highly recommended. I had gone without help for several weeks while waiting until she was available to work for us. Later in the day an old Vietnamese man pushing a two-wheel cart came for our former servant's belongings, and she disappeared forever. Shortly afterward, an embassy security team came by, and our night guard left without saying good-bye, replaced by a Vietnamese who would not even let my husband in the gate without him showing proper ID.

I guess the moral of the story is that even with sixteen years of Catholic education, mostly in girls' schools, you can wind up running a whore house if you do not watch your step!

More Than One Way To Kill A Germ

We had a misunderstanding with our cook that nearly poisoned us. All fruits and vegetables in Manila had to be soaked in a disinfectant product called Milton. One evening we were having dinner and the spinach had a foul medicinal taste and odor to it. I asked the cook if she had cleaned the spinach properly and she assured me she had. "You soaked it in Milton?" I asked. "Well," she answered, "we ran out of Milton, but I did soak it for an hour in something just as good!" I asked her to show me and it was Lysol Disinfectant. Got to give it to her, it did have disinfectant on the label. But it tasted awful!

Polish It Until It Shines

When we hired our first cook, Ah Yang, we explained to him that he would be required to keep the kitchen clean, which included all the utensils, the linens, the brass pieces, silver, and china. The first week, Ah Yang tried to do his best and to do everything he was supposed to do. Therefore, I was not surprised when he gave me a list of things to buy at the commissary that included steel wool pads and scouring powder. But imagine my dismay and consternation a couple of days later when I noticed deep scratches on my silver centerpiece. He had conscientiously and diligently removed all the tarnish from all the silver and brass with steel wool and scouring powder. He did it innocently and, although most of the silver has been refinished, some pieces still bear scratches. They are memories of a good cook and a nice person and a first-tour wife who learned the hard way to give detailed directions to servants.

Hot Stuff

One evening, about a half-hour before we were expecting eight of Bill's Vietnamese and American business associates to arrive for dinner, we heard a crescendo of hysterical screams from the kitchen. Rushing down the stairs, we found a propane cylinder rolling in circles on the floor and flames filling the room. With terror fueling his adrenaline, Bill wrestled the ten-pound monster out the back door. I dashed across the street to the nearest telephone. I contacted the fire station but immediately discovered that we had no common language. Miming would not work this time, and I hung up in frustration, returning home to find the fire out and cylinder spewing its last flames outside the house. Fortunately, the only damage was one burned curtain, much grimy soot, and a lingering smell.

Dinner preparations were completed in a neighbor's kitchen.

Sweets Before Salt

Late in our first tour in Taiwan, we were invited by our neighbors for dinner and bridge. They had just hired a new cook, Ah Wu, and were in the process of training him for meal planning, preparation, and entertaining. Sheila, our hostess, told Ah Wu what she would like him to prepare for dinner. She asked him if he knew how to prepare the dish as an entree, and because he had come to her with good recommendations as a very experienced cook, she was not surprised when he assured her that he needed no instructions to prepare the menu she had requested.

After cocktails, Ah Wu appeared at the living room door in his impeccable white jacket, bowed, and announced that dinner was served. We seated ourselves, ate our salads, then waited for the main course. Ah Wu proudly came through the kitchen door bearing a pie covered with beautiful, fluffy meringue, which he placed in front of our host. With a perplexed expression on her face, Sheila looked at him, smiled, and motioned for Ah Wu to come to her chair. We heard her say, "Ah Wu, don't you know that dessert is served at the end of the meal and not after the salad?" With an equally puzzled look on his face, Ah Wu softly said, "But Missy, you said that you wanted chicken pot pie for the main dish." And it was delicious.

The Joys of Household Help

In Manila, we hired Rosie and Gloria, twin sisters from Mindanao. They were in their late teens, but Rosie was already a fairly accomplished cook. I showed her some of our favorite recipes, and she did well. We planned an important dinner party to entertain some other diplomats and she and I discussed the menu, which ended with a wonderful chocolate cake for dessert. The dinner went well and everyone had a good time. Gloria came through the swinging door with a cake about one inch high! It was three layers, but each layer looked like a matzoh. I went out to the kitchen to ask Rosie about the cake. She told me that she had run out of flour, so she substituted corn starch. After all, she had sometimes used corn starch to thicken sauces instead of flour, so she thought there would be no problem using it for the cake. What was funny is that she had taken the trouble to frost each layer. We had fruit for dessert.

One New Year's Day in Bangkok, we were invited to a friend's house for brunch. She called me at about ten in the morning requesting that I bring as many eggs as I had and to call some of the others who were coming and ask them to bring as many eggs as *they* had. We got to her house and asked her what had happened. It seems that early in the morning, she had sent her maid to the market to buy thirty eggs, and the maid had not returned. We all had brought more than enough eggs to scramble, so she went into the kitchen to start preparing the brunch. A few minutes later, the gate bell rang and she went to answer the bell. There stood her maid with five men behind, and each one was carrying six dozen eggs. She had bought thirty dozen eggs and told Madame that the next time Madame needed so many eggs, she should tell her ahead of time so that she could order them.

Another friend "lived on the economy" in Bangkok, which meant she did not have commissary privileges because her husband was a contractor in Vietnam. She had returned from home leave in the States and brought back an electric frying pan with teflon coating. In 1968 this was a new innovation, and everyone wanted a frying pan like this. She was proud of the pan and gave it to her cook to use. She came home not too many days later to find her driver scrubbing all the teflon out of the pan; he very proudly held up the teflon-less pan and told Madame that he had been able to clean it up! Needless to say, my friend went into the house and had a very stiff drink of Scotch.

Our first maid in Bangkok was a very young woman from the Klong Toei section of town. This is the fishing port and a very poor area. She spoke no English and I did not speak Thai, but with sign language, I was able to tell her what needed to be done. She was the number two which meant she did the laundry (by hand, no washing machine), ironing, cleaning, and baby-sitting with our daughter. When I asked her what her name was, she told me "Mai Ma." We just loved her. She always wore a smile and, despite the language barrier, she was "number one" in our book. Eventually, I started teaching her English. We started out with the basics and we got to the point where I said to her one day: "My Name is Madame Karen and your name is Mai Ma." To which she responded, "No." I asked "No?" and she repeated "No." I took her down to the telephone operator of the apartment building where we lived and I asked her to ask Mai Ma just what her name was. Mai Ma told her "Noi." I could not get over it because this was several months after she had started working for us and, we had been calling her "Mai Ma" all this time. Mai Ma in Thai means "Don't Come." Strangely, after we started calling her "Noi," she stopped smiling and eventually did not show up one day. According to the telephone operator, who was the major domo of all the maids in the apartment building, Noi thought that Mai

Ma was our pet name for her and that it meant we liked her. When we started calling her Noi, she thought that we no longer liked or wanted her. We asked the operator to tell her that we still liked her, but she never came back.

Next we hired Bunlong who came highly recommended. She was to be our number one and would do all the cooking and shopping for us at local markets. Bunlong had been trained by a Cordon Bleu chef and was very good. My family has never eaten as well as we did when we had Bunlong. In addition to being a fantastic cook, Bunlong spoke English and took excellent care of our daughter, as well as the other children in our apartment building. We relied on her for her intelligence, wit, and common sense. Bunlong was the one who asked me never to speak Thai outside because, as she explained it to me, she knew what I meant but she was afraid others might not and that I might say something offensive. I always appreciated her candor, and know that she probably saved me from making a fool of myself. Bunlong spoiled us all.

My husband was on a long trip, and I had gotten up early one morning to get my daughter off to school. I did not feel good and I told Pathin, our number two, that I was going back to bed for a while. I was supposed to play bridge, but when Bunlong came to awaken me, she could not rouse me. She went to my neighbor's and asked Carol to come and awaken Madame. Carol came and realized that I had a high fever from the flu and was incoherent. She rushed me to the hospital, where I slept for four days, and only after I recovered did I find out that during the entire time, Bunlong slept on the floor beside my bed in case I needed anything. I've always thought that that was the kindest thing anyone has ever done for me.

Thi Hai—Guardian of Children

We arrived in Saigon the fifth day of 1963—a tumultuous year in that lovely country. The *bonzes* (Buddhist monks) burning themselves in the streets, the raiding of the pagodas, Madame Nhu, three American ambassadors in the next two years, constant coup attempts or rumors, the generals' coup d'etat which overthrew Ngo Dinh Diem and, three weeks later, the assassination in Dallas. All that notwithstanding, we enjoyed that tour as much as any we'd ever had.

This story is about our amah, Thi Hai. In Vietnam, girls often were numbered in lieu of a name, and thus she was known as Daughter Number One. In June 1963 our second son, Christopher, was born at Dr. Tran Dinh De's Clinic at 179 Rue Cong Ly, the launching pad for a lot of American children in that era. Thi Hai was unmarried, fortyish, broad-beamed, and probably destined to end her days taking care of her aged mother. She virtually adopted Christopher—we began to worry he would never learn to walk since she did all her chores with him perched on her hip. On November 1, 1963, I was at the US Navy Clinic to visit our eldest son, Eric, who had been kept overnight because of a fever. My husband was at the American Embassy, then in the old building near the river. In a matter of hours, the city erupted with the coup d'etat, and we found ourselves marooned, tanks rumbling through the streets and artillery fire raining down on the city from outside. All travel was impossible for many hours. At that time, very few of us had telephones at home. We would send messages via "amah-courier," go ourselves, or just wait until we saw someone the next day. During the coup we had no way of contacting our own house, where Thi Hai had been left to take care of Christopher for what was supposed to be a couple of hours but had turned into a day. Would she panic and take off? Would she take her infant charge with her, or perhaps worse, would she leave him there alone?

The streets were alive with the sound of gunfire, tanks, and soldiers running everywhere. Finally there came a call to my husband from his boss's wife, Stephane; Thi Hai had just appeared at her house, several blocks from our house on Rue Pasteur, carrying a well-swaddled Christopher. Stephane said, *"Magnifique, Thi Hai! Emmenez-Christophe dans la salon."* ("Wonderful, Thi Hai! Bring Christopher into the living room.") But Thi Hai insisted on keeping her young charge with her, so Christopher spent the coup in the amah's quarters at the rear of the house, still clutched in Thi Hai's arms. She had realized that my husband's boss had a phone and had carried the child through the side streets to his house.

Eric is now a stockbroker in California and Christopher a real estate executive in Dallas; and, of course, neither of them remembers any of this. That said, we all hope very much that Thi Hai is happy and well in Vietnam, or wherever she may be.

Hostess with the Mostest

In the good old days when the east was wild, we returned from a dinner hosted by the chief of station (COS) for the visiting division chief. For cover reasons we had not taken our own car but had been picked up and taken home by another guest. We had no sooner gone upstairs and undressed for bed when our gate bell rang and we could hear our guard arguing with someone. My husband went out to see what was amiss. He came back in and called the marine guard and the COS. The person at the gate was a foreign national carrying a briefcase and demanding to see the "US official who lives here." It was obvious that he had been waiting for us to return home. The guard had locked the gate but was afraid that the man had a gun. The COS, the visiting division chief, and a marine contingent arrived all at once. One of the marines and the COS talked to the man while the division chief asked my husband if he had a gun. "Right here," my husband said, pulling a pistol from his bathrobe pocket. "Son, give me the gun before you blow your balls off, and go put some pants on," he told my husband and took the pistol, tucking it into his trouser waistband. My husband dressed and went back downstairs, only to return a few minutes later to ask me to make some coffee and bring some after dinner drinks out to the verandah. After an "are you (expletive deleted) nuts?" I served the guests including the "gentleman who needed to see the American official" drinks and snacks at 3:00 A.M. before they all went for a little ride in the COS's car at the gentleman's request. It seems he had developed a drug problem while studying in a rival Cold War country and went a little off every so often. "He had important papers to show the Americans," but first he wanted to ride around and listen to the cassette player. Just another harmless looney and just another evening of being hostess with the mostest!

Malesh, My Foot

As I walked out the back kitchen door, I looked down to see broken glass all over the stoop. I called the nanny to ask why the broken glass shards were left there. She admitted that she had broken a glass and had swept it out the kitchen door. When I commented how dangerous that could be, especially with a toddler around, she said "*Malesh.*" I went nuts! How dare she say *malesh*, which means no big deal or it doesn't matter! I went around ranting and raving until the cook came to ask what was going on. I explained and he answered "*malesh*" as well! I was ready to fire both of them. I later found out quite by accident that *malesh* also means "I am sorry" and that both of them had been trying to say that they regretted not cleaning up the shards. Other nations, other languages.

Army of Pigs

I think back now and remember how brave, naive, or both I was when, at twenty-eight, I hosted a cocktail party for 185 people to meet and greet our replacements as we prepared to leave our first post. Of course, Murphy's law took over and our replacements did not arrive on the scheduled day. I had hired two extra cooks from the deputy chief of mission's (DCM) residence to help prepare the food. I had spent many days cooking and freezing cocktail party fare. The head cook assured me that we had enough food for an army. However, the party did not thin out, and as the food began to disappear, I entered the kitchen to tell the cooks that we needed to replenish the food. "It is gone," said Gamel. I replied, "I thought that you said that we had enough for an army!"

"An army of soldiers, yes. You have an army of pigs!" And yes, the guests had truly enjoyed the food, but by 9 P.M. we were really scrounging for cheese, crackers, and whatever the two neighbors above us had in their larders. It did not seem to bother a number of guests who decided to stay until the booze ran out. At 1 A.M. it did, and the party moved to another house. We came home at 4 A.M. Two hours later, the telephone rang and we answered it to find out that our replacements had arrived in the middle of the night. Too bad they missed the longest cocktail party we have ever had and the "army of pigs."

Baby of the House

At some posts, one is lucky enough to inherit well-trained help. Such was the case when my husband arrived as the new chief of station (COS). By the time my children and I came a month later, the cook and his wife had everything under control. Along with the cook and his wife, we also inherited their six children. Most days, there were few problems; however, our dog, knowing that one of the little boys was petrified of dogs, helped him train for the Olympics by chasing him from gate to door. During our last year at post, their seventeen-year-old daughter became pregnant. One day, when my husband was meeting with the ambassador, he received an emergency phone call from home. When he answered, the cook told him that his daughter was having difficulty delivering the baby—my husband informed the cook that he was not a midwife and he suggested to the cook that he take his daughter to the hospital. Later he felt guilty and when he called home, he was told that the baby had arrived and he could name it, as was the custom. As luck would have it, the regional medical officer was visiting and having dinner with us that evening. We all looked at the newest member of our family as the regional medical officer checked her. We named her in spite of my husband's resistance to the idea, but it was either we name her or she would be named after my husband. We asked the cook to go and buy a layette—our treat. I often came home from work to find my daughter playing with the baby and announcing that she needed to adopt her. I must admit that I often think of our little foster granddaughter and hope that she is well and happy.

Chapter V

"SEX, LIES AND THE SHRINKING BIRD DISEASE"

Excerpt from The Saigon Post, South Vietnam
circa 1966

Saigon. Vietnamese medical doctors recently met with representatives of the American Embassy to discuss the infiltration of an unknown disease into South Vietnam. The Vietnamese males have accused the American GI of bringing a heretofore unknown condition called "the Shrinking Bird Disease" into their country. The GIs have been known to frequent prostitutes and bar girls. The disease is being passed to the Vietnamese males from the bar girls and prostitutes. Vietnamese men are lamenting the fact that their penises (called "birds" in slang) are shrinking. The American Embassy had no comment.

Hidden Passion

It was a hot, sultry day in Asia. I was sitting on the steps of the marine house talking to one of the marines. My husband, a case officer, was on yet another TDY. I was bored with overseas life. I was bored with him. He was running from affair to affair with the station secretaries, and I knew about it. But what could I do, so far from home with small children, maids, and too much time to think. Here was this adorable young marine-tall and sexy and looking for love! I was in my late thirties, short and sexy and looking for anything! For the sake of anonymity, I will call my marine, Jay—he was one of America's fine young men—guardian of freedom at the gates of communism.

We had the token conversation about overseas life and the perils of this place. I threw caution to the wind, didn't consider the consequences. He was bored, had done the secretary routine—obviously the secretaries at this post had no lack of bed partners.

And so it all began, like right that moment. I looked into those big brown eyes and off we ran. To the freight elevator in the marine house! He planned to sneak me into his room but we couldn't wait. With a frenzy, we tore at our clothes, stopped the elevator between floors, and consummated our relationship without a care for anything else. It was the beginning of a beautiful year.

We took chances all the time, swimming out to a raft in the South China Sea in the middle of the night in shark-filled waters; dinners by moonlight on remote beaches; making love on the ninth green of an exclusive golf and country club with a spotlight roaming overhead; ferry boat rides to beautiful hotels on remote islands. We could not stay away from each other. He was like an aphrodisiac to my body and soul.

The really dangerous times were when he let me into the consulate at night when he was on duty. We would go into one of the offices and make love on the couch or desk. One evening we even went into the "bubble," a totally secure area where conversations were scrambled and where they had the most bee-uu-ti-ful conference table, perfect for a night of passion. I got a bit paranoid over that one, especially when I had to go to a meeting in there the next morning. I was working as a contract wife for the station. So we gave that spot up because I had a difficult time focusing on the discussion at hand—my mind kept wandering back to the night with Jay! There did not seem to be a spot in the consulate where we had not marked our turf, so to speak.

It was all so crazy. Half of the thrill was making love in places where we could be discovered at any given moment. But at the time, we thought we were in love. Who knows, maybe we were. I look back now, having worked through my guilt, divorced and comfortable in my own skin, and I wonder at how I could have taken such chances. It was a relationship that was important to my survival at the time. I could not have dealt with the loneliness and the pain of being somewhere that I did not want to be without this union with Jay. I don't know where Jay is today, but it really doesn't matter. I have special memories of stolen moments and they are delicious.

Booze and Boys

We arrived in Bangkok at the height of the Vietnam war, and there were a lot of young servicemen in town. Wherever we went, young men would be whistling and flirting with us. The officers' club was a great place to hang out and meet and talk and drink with these brave young men who would soon return to the maelstrom. Shortly after I arrived, one of the senior officer's wives took me aside and told me that the only way to get through the days of overseas life was either "booze, bennies, or boys" or a combination of any two and sometimes all three. I thought to myself how sad it was that we had to use this to get through these lush tropical days. I had not yet faced life with servants and a lot of time on my hands. Time to play bridge, have lunch, play some more bridge, and eventually add mah jong to fill the hours. It sounded like so much fun—how could anyone be bored? I had a cook and a number two who did all of the housework and the laundry. I only had to get myself up each day, dress, eat, go to the beauty parlor. What luxury!

Then boredom and ennui set in. When I reflect on this today, I wonder why I had no hobby or some inner resource to help me. I was ill-prepared for overseas life. I had gone from my mother's home to my marriage home and had never really taken any time to find out who I was or what was inside of me. Back in the early sixties, very few women were encouraged to reflect on their innermost feelings or thoughts. But then I guess very few men were either. We just moved from day to day and, of course, as long as you were in the US, we were so busy taking care of home and family that we never thought about—or had—any free time. Now suddenly I had free time and no way to fill the hours and I had no small children to occupy the space.

I learned to drink and found out that vodka and tonics go a long way in easing boredom and loneliness. It sounds ridiculous to say that one could be lonely while being with friends and playing bridge and having luncheons and attending cocktail parties. Our husbands were off playing 007 and all sorts of exciting things like flying up into the northern part of Laos in helicopters or meeting their agents in clandestine safehouses. They had all sorts of games to keep them busy: playing Cowboys and Indians with live ammunition. I used to get up and hear myself say, "Oh God, another beautiful day!"

So life became a blur, one day flowing into the next. No margins, no stops, no parameters. It was up to each individual to establish these, and I quickly discovered that I was not equipped to do so; or maybe, to be honest, I did not want to. It was easier to just blend each day into an alcoholic haze. We had bloody marys in the morning, drank wine with lunch, and then on to vodka and tonics for the balance of the day. Thus my introduction into the booze part of the equation.

Next for me was the boys. I soon discovered that western women were very attractive to the fly boys from Vietnam as well as the Filipino musicians. I hate to use the disclaimer that I was lonely or that my husband did not pay much attention to me or that the alcohol made it easier. The bottom line was that I enjoyed being the object of flirtation. It was fun to slow dance with someone and have him respond to my body movements. Today it sounds so shallow and pathetic, but at the time, it certainly filled a lot of hours. By my second tour in Asia, I was well into the boys. I enjoyed it all and never took the time to think of the pain I was causing in my husband. It was more important to me to satisfy this hunger within me—I needed the attention of other men. By now I had graduated to martinis and I can remember thinking of how cool it all was, drinking martinis and smoking cigarettes. It was positively mind-boggling that this girl from the Midwest would be doing all of this in an exotic city in the Far East. It seemed so sophisticated. After all, we were hobnobbing with the elite in each country that we lived in—powerful politicians, rich families who lived in homes that I had only read about, and some of these men found me exciting! How exhilarating it all was. I continued this pattern until I arrived in Hong Kong, where I was fortunate enough to meet some women who introduced me to feminism. It is amazing that all it took was for me to attend a consciousness raising group, and I realized suddenly that I did not like myself the way I was or what I was doing to myself and my family. I had learned to rationalize my actions by thinking that I was only doing what others were doing, and I had used that excuse for several years. I have always been grateful that I met these women at a time in my life when I still had the opportunity to change and grow.

After much soul searching, I came to understand that I had to learn to fill my hours of the day more appropriately. I had enjoyed the thrill of the courtship, the secret rendezvous, but I knew that I could not continue on this path. Too many people were in danger of being badly hurt by my actions. Only I could kick the alcohol and the boy habit. Alcohol had served the purpose of being my tranquilizer and enough was enough.

Today I see young women going overseas who are so much better prepared than we were. Back in the fifties and sixties, women were just expected to be part of the household effects that were sent overseas along with the case officer. Luckily the young wives of today receive some training and a lot of information. Additionally between CNN and other satellites and the advent of computers and e-mail, life overseas is no longer as remote as it once was. I have no regrets for myself—I am only grateful that I could stop the spinning before it destroyed me, my husband and my family. Whenever someone remarks to me that they think that I am so together, I have to laugh and remember that it was not always so.

Bald-Faced Lies and Cambodian Skirts

We were in Manila for quite some time before I realized that my husband was frequenting every whorehouse known to man. It took me a long time to figure out that the term "I'm going to the massage parlor" actually meant "I'm going to get laid"!

He showed up with a pretty Filipina and introduced her as Josie, a gal "related to one of the locals who worked in Logistics." He said that she needed a job. We already had two maids, a sew girl, a gardener, and a driver, and I could not figure out what Josie could do for us. However, Dick had already told her that she could live with us and had all her belongings and a cot in the trunk of the car, so she moved in to the maids' quarters. Since I was hardly ever home myself, I did not realize that Dick had moved his concubine in under my roof. I found out later that he put her through two years of business school while she lived with us. I guess this was Dick's very own Marshall Plan project.

After our return to the States, he came home one evening and announced that he wanted to take me out to dinner. I got a sitter, and he took me to the Montgomery Mall Hot Shoppes Cafeteria: the last of the big-time spenders! In this modest setting, Dick told me that the agency was sending him to Cambodia on TDY for six weeks. He did not want to go, but he had to do his duty. So off he went, leaving me behind with two small children. The TDY got longer and longer. I began hearing stories from friends in Phnom Penh that he was misbehaving, a euphemism for screwing his brains out. When he finally got home seven months later, he had lost about thirty pounds and looked like a zombie. His behavior was, let's say, unconventional. He walked around the house with those long Cambodian skirts on, no shirt or shoes, listening to some strange Cambodian music on the stereo and burning incense.

Things were pretty sick around the house with incense burning, Cambodian soul music, and the skirt. Finally one day, he came home from work and told me that he had to return to Cambodia for another six months. I found out later that he had called in every IOU in order to go back to Cambodia. So off he went, and the calls home became further and further apart, but the war was winding down and life was pretty hectic there, and I thought that this was the reason.

He called me from Cambodia and told me that he had this great idea about bringing home this Cambodian woman who would like to come to America and work for me. Even I woke up on that one. He planned to put her in our downstairs den and she would be the maid. I refused the generous offer.

The war ended in 1975 and Dick returned to the States. Unbeknownst to me, Dick brought his little girlfriend, Nora, with him. He left her in San Francisco in the relocation center and came home to suburban Maryland. Dick had lost most of his hair, looked gray, and was a nervous wreck. One day, while he was at the office, his girlfriend called me from San Francisco and asked for Mr. Dick. I asked who she was and she answered, "I work for Mr. Dick in Phnom Penh. I cold here, you send me coat?"

The next day he said he had to go to San Francisco on TDY and left without packing. For twenty days, I did not hear from him, and one day I called his office in Langley to inquire if he was in fact still alive. That night at midnight, he called me and announced that he wanted a divorce. Needless to say, I fell off my chair.

By 1 A.M., I had a lawyer and detective lined up, and three days later when Mr. Dick and his darling Nora arrived at Dulles, the detective was clicking away with his camera. Dick put the girl up in a furnished apartment in Silver Spring, the same apartment complex that we had stayed in after our first overseas tour. I sent the detective over-click click click. Very soon Dick was told to get his girlfriend on the first plane back to California.

He was one lonely, miserable son of a bitch. The lawyer told me to get as much information as I could, so I went into high gear with my mother who was quite adept at photographing pictures and copying letters, TSD (Technical Services Division) style.

One night after Dick had fallen asleep (or so I thought), I went through his wallet and found her picture in a secret pocket. I took it downstairs and photographed it with the Polaroid, put it back, and went on more searches: coat pockets, pants pockets, etc. Luckily I came across the sweetest little letter from Miss Nora and it was unsealed. I scurried off to Xerox it and put it back.

After a while, I think Dick realized that his dream of having this Cambodian cutie for a wife ("she makes me feel like a butterfly floating through air") was pretty much a lost cause and apparently he wrote her a "Dear Jane" letter. She tore it to pieces, and put it in an envelope together with *treasures* and a letter, calling him a "dumb bustard" and telling him he was full of "chit." The box of her beloved memories arrived: toys from Cracker Jack boxes, five-and-dime junk jewelry, and amusement park coins that were stamped "Dick and Nora". His returned *"Dear Jane"* letter was a real corker about how he could not marry her because he had "responsibilities at home, but he knew she would find happiness with someone else. He was only so sorry that it had to end."

I decided that it would not be over until I was ready. I had seen too many of my friends live in near poverty following a divorce and I was determined that this would not be my fate. I made my plans, raised my children, and got into a position where I would not have to trade down my lifestyle. It was not easy and it certainly was painful, but I was determined to do it on my terms.

* * *

After our Cambodian fiasco, we were assigned to Headquarters for almost three years and Dick was miserable. Too many people stateside did not agree with his philosophy of "if it is wearing a skirt and moves, jump on it." Finally, after bugging everyone he knew who could help him, a tour to Berlin came up. He was thrilled.

I actually had been making plans to get rid of him, but the timing was not right. I had no skills that would help me in job hunting so I had to bite the bullet and bide my time, so off to Berlin. No one had a clue that we were definitely headed for divorce somewhere down the line. We looked like the all-American family coming to Berlin and fitting in.

Berlin for Dick was more "fun and games" but this time, he pursued women in the office. One woman would brazenly call our home at 3 A.M. She was replaced by a twenty-four-year-old TDYer. When summer came, I packed up the children, mailed a few extra boxes of clothing, took my jewelry, and left for home. Dick stayed on in Berlin for another year.

Well, he finally came back home, only to discover that we had adjusted to life without him, and it created all sorts of problems. I found out that Dick was taking a new flame to my now deceased mother's condominium for his Friday night "cock" tail hour. The next Saturday morning he was up bright and early making his mess of scrambled eggs and I sat in the rocker, just rocking very slowly and confronted him. Well, he turned gray and green at the same time and began yelling. The rocking ceased, and I made the decision that it was time for a divorce. I had held out as long as it suited me. He had to get out. And out he went. Never even cleaned up the frying pan of messy scrambled eggs.

We got divorced and he went off on another tour, where he met his new wife. He never bothered to tell her that he would only be receiving half of his retirement (the other half was mine by Act of Congress), and retirement day arrived. His new trophy wife suddenly realized that even a senior officer's retirement does not go very far when it is only half! She called my daughter to see if I had any plans to marry soon or maybe even die. The last time I checked, I did not plan to remarry, since I had not even been dating yet, and dying definitely was not an option. I felt that I was just starting to live. I have kept my sense of humor and now I have been given the opportunity to tell my story. Good God, I am free at last!

Chapter VI

HAPPY HOLIDAYS

Long before the telephone came to the Third World and the Internet was just a dream in cyberspace, we were overseas with no close family. We brought our traditions with us and tried to adapt them to the countries we were posted to. We substituted ingredients with what was available. Our friends became our extended families and we celebrated the holidays with them. In fact, for many of us, we still celebrate the holidays with our immediate families and our extended families. They have blended into one.

For some of us who were posted in countries or cities where travel was limited, we needed to find ways to unwind. We hosted theme parties, and there was always someone new to post who could teach us the latest dance crazes. Our husbands were working endless days and nights and we were under the pressure of holding families together in exotic and sometimes dangerous posts. The parties gave us an opportunity to bond with each other and just have fun.

Three Happy Holidays

It was our first Christmas married and our first tour overseas. Here we were in Danang, South Vietnam. Young, idealistic, scared, and excited at the same time. We had another American couple living next door who had three children. Somehow, when you are overseas, you form bonds that are unbreakable, permanent. Christmas is difficult at best when you are in a foreign land and away from immediate family. We were determined to make the most of it.

Toys

Toys for the kids next door? They had been ordered from Sears and were to arrive at the APO in Saigon. One of our case officers had offered to make sure that the packages were put on the weekly courier flight up to Danang. The flight came and we went out to meet it on Christmas Eve. No packages. No toys for Christmas! Not even a tape of *Miracle on 34th Street* to make us feel a little better. What to do? Call the station in Saigon. It was 4 P.M. They were all at the *Cosmos Club* downstairs from the office, partying. We got one of the marine guards to go down and get one of the officers. Toys? They are here in the registry room on the floor. We forgot them. Thanks a lot.

We pondered for hours. Surely there was something we could do. Tell the kids it was next week? No, they were too smart for that. We got more and more morose as the evening wore on. It was raining outside. The markets were closed, so we couldn't even find a Vietnamese toy at this late hour. There was a knock on the door about 11 P.M. There in the pouring rain stood one of the army pilots from Danang Air Base who was on duty that night. In his Jeep were all the packages with "Sears Roebuck" marked on the side! The case officer who was at the *Cosmos Club* had driven them out to Tan Son Nhut airport. He pleaded his case, and one of the military planes that was bringing ammunition to Danang agreed to take on some extra cargo. His aircraft became a Santa sled! The majority of the toys were "some assembly required" (which we all know means that it will take anyone over the age of ten at least four hours to assemble), but we finally finished at about 5 A.M. and they were all under the tree just like Santa would have put them.

Trees

There were no Christmas trees for sale at the Buddhist temple across from our house in Danang. My husband left for his trip down to Hoi An that Christmas Eve morning. I was resigned to the fact that we would not have a Christmas tree. I had decorated the house in fine style with items purchased at the PX in Saigon. My husband was late getting home that night, and I was concerned as it was a dangerous drive. I heard him at the gate and ran to the door. There in the back of the Jeep were two of the skinniest, scrawniest scrub pine trees I had ever seen! It seems that my sentimental spouse had taken his Jeep along with his interpreter out on the beach, where they cut down the trees. While they were cutting the trees, a large group of villagers appeared from nowhere, as they are prone to do in Southeast Asia. My husband and Ky, the interpreter, loaded the two trees in the Jeep and started up the hill back to the road. No luck. They were stuck in the sand. The villagers just stood there and look puzzled. The sun was going down. This was a very dangerous area after dark. All of a sudden, the villagers got behind the Jeep and pushed it out. Ky was very nervous on the drive back, as it was getting dark very quickly. "What is wrong?" my husband asked.

"You should really be grateful that those people helped you," he explained. "They are from a Viet Cong village that is not friendly to foreigners after the sun goes down."

The branches from the two trees were wired together and it was the most beautiful Christmas tree we ever had!

Turkey

We were invited out Thanksgiving night to the province chief's house. Now in Danang, there was little housing that Americans are used to. There were French villas for the rich and shacks for the rest. The province chief lived in a shack with three small children, who came to greet us at the door. We could not converse with them. We had not taken our interpreter with us for this social occasion, so we sat and stared at each other. They laughed a lot which Vietnamese are prone to do when they are nervous. Finally, the wife appeared in the door of this apparently one-room home. We were sitting on a couch, and she brought in two small end tables, one lower than the other, and covered them with a cloth. They teetered about as she placed two small covered bowls on them. They asked us to "eat"—the one word they knew in English. We lifted the tops off the bowls and there snuggled together were six small snails in each bowl. Try using chopsticks when you haven't really mastered the art and eating snails when you don't like them, all the while with five pairs of eyes watching you struggle. We did it. They were so grateful to entertain us for our holiday that they never ate. They had only enough money to pay for our meal. A true holiday gift.

The Party

I could smell it before I could see it: stale beer, damp smoky air leavened with a mix of salt, cheese, and sweat. My mouth tasted like a dust bunny deep fried in Listerine. The clock struck seven, four hours since my spouse and I had waved good night to the last happy, if disoriented, guest.

I picked my way through the cups and ashtrays (smoking was a social crime in those days, not a political one) to the kitchen, where I fumbled with the coffee maker. My poor brain was receiving two alternating messages: what a party, need coffee, what a party, need coffee. I was suppressing the knowledge that this was Sunday and, more important, the amah's day off, which meant my spouse and I were on our own with the clean up. I glanced at the sink. A wine cork that clearly bore teeth marks was floating in the dishwater.

I took my coffee and Sunday paper and walked to the balcony at the end of the living room. There was nothing broken that I could see, but there was a large damp area on the carpet. "Communal shampoo" flashed across my dying frontal lobes. I eased open the door so as not to waken my spouse and settled into the corner chair.

It was one of those gorgeous fall days we sometimes got in Hong Kong when the breeze off the South China Sea blew out the dust and smog and presented picture-book China—batwing junks gliding between small islands on calm blue water. The breeze felt good on my temples, and the coffee began to clear my head.

Our flat was in Repulse Bay on the back side of Hong Kong island. It overlooked a popular beach on which, now that my eyes were focusing, I could see an unusual amount of activity. There was a large crowd of Chinese standing in a disorganized circle staring at a large blue-black mass on the beach. The bluc-black mass was actually a female mass in a blue dress and a male mass dressed in black, both of whom had been upright and no worse for wear than their pie-eyed host and hostess when they'd waved goodbye in the wee small hours. They were clearly entangled but seemed to be fully clothed and happy in their own garments. It was an unusual pairing, however. The blue dress was one of our very own officers, a full-figured, worldly wise veteran of a spontaneous nature. A true collector of strays, she had gathered in a young (much younger) oh-so-very-serious, first tour State officer, who now slept on her generous bosom. The Chinese seemed puzzled but genuinely amused and, being Cantonese, they continued eating, depositing bits of chicken feet and Godknowswhat around the slumbering couple. I had two thoughts: They are far enough from the water so they won't drown; and I need an aspirin.

* * *

Thinking back on the party after all these years, I can say that nothing truly scandalous occurred. Everyone (mostly) stayed dressed (mostly) and everyone (with perhaps one exception) went home with the person he or she came with. It was lively and perhaps even naughty, but in a Iowa-Rotarians-on-convention sort of way, a what-the-hell-let's-order-another-round-of-drinks-that-look-like-blue-tidy-bowls-with-umbrellas-cause-the-folks-back-in-Davenport-will-never-know-anyway night. We walked that fine line between *what a great party* and *see you in court*.

Still, there is the question of how a group of generally conservative, well-behaved adults in their thirties and forties suddenly ended up in a communal shampoo. It may have something to do with being East of Suez. The mystic Orient does cast a spell and, while we have given up white linen suits and ceiling fans, that is not true for gin and tonic. The mysterious East has a sensuous quality that works its way into your bones. Couple that with a full moon, rock fever (it was almost impossible to leave Hong Kong in those days), and months of very long hours that strained family life as a number of sensitive operations moved into critical stages, and you have a situation where everyone was feeling the pressure and in desperate need of an opportunity to relieve it. It undoubtedly helped that traffic was awful that night, so people were late and exhausted by the time they arrived, that my husband shoved a drink in their hand the moment they walked in the door, and that dinner was very late getting to the table.

The party was my idea. It was a way to say thank you to the large number of people who had gone out of their way to embrace a young couple who had just had their first child and were very far from family and friends. US diplomatic missions are like small towns. There are rivalries and strains, but people tend to pull together and support one another, and that was certainly true for us during our first year abroad. I wanted our party to be special and a bit silly, so in honor of my spouse's Scandinavian heritage, I decided we would celebrate Leif Erikson Day, which as far as I know is not celebrated even in Scandinavia.

The guest list was unusual, too. For one thing, it was larger than most. We invited almost fifty people, and it represented a cross-section of the mission: agency officers, state officers, the defense attaches, and even a few stray foreign diplomats, including a visitor from the Dutch Embassy in Beijing who became more confused, not to say disoriented, as the evening went on. We purposely avoided inviting the more senior people in the consulate, figuring people would be more likely to relax without them.

I was the party's mother, but two close friends, "my sisters," were its heart and soul. We were not real sisters, of course, but we often did things together and had grown close as people in difficult circumstances often do. Looking back after all these years, I realize we were fine when separate, but when together something took over. We became silly. We fed off one another and like the Three Witches in Macbeth, drove the action wherever we were. Now, I confess that I was the most deceptive of the three. I looked every bit the well-mannered new mom fresh from middle America. But I am also prone to the impulsive act when given a nudge, and so was the first sister, the Pixie, good at providing that little push that launched me and sent her into gales of laughter punctuated by "oh no." The second sister had a feline grace and a laugh that suggested she knew more than you did and was just waiting for you to realize it. She seemed to float above and apart, touching down now and then to give encouragement, make a telling observation, or push the action forward.

On the night of the party, our flat looked great. Novelist John LeCarre once described the post as looking like it was furnished by Howard Johnson's, and most of the post's flats had that flavor about them as well. Our place was less institutional. I have a decorator's eye, and I used it to good effect in Hong Kong's small shops. We had also shipped a number of our own things, including a grandfather clock that chimed on the quarter hour, and a large square coffee table that dominated the living room. It was set with a grand floral display. Our place looked more like a home than most and it sparkled. I am a ferocious housekeeper. You can eat off our floors; good thing too, because I think that the cheese ball ended up there a couple of times.

The dining room table was laid with our best linen cloth (purchased that very day from the China Fleet Club), and we had every variety of odd food and condiments that the small commissary had to offer: pickled herring, artichoke hearts, Japanese crackers, dry salted peas, and so forth. All of which, come to think of it, tended to make people thirstier. And we had that one covered. My husband had laid in a variety of distilled spirits, a keg of beer, and two bottles of Danish aquavit—a fiery caraway flavored alcohol—that sat chilled and on the table bracketing another floral centerpiece. Add to this the wine that a number of guests brought, and we were well watered. The amah was running late with the main courses, but we had a variety of dishes for people to select from. I even baked a couple of cheesecakes for dessert.

Traffic was awful and the guests were delayed. I rarely drink, but I was on my second drink when the first guest arrived, the Very Serious Young Diplomat, or VSYD. The invitation said casual, but there he was in a dark suit and tie. The VSYD did not have the mildly constipated look that young State officers were encouraged to affect, but he did have a state department name; his first name was a last name and his last name was a first name. This would be comical if it were not so common throughout the department. I have visions of all the poor, unfortunate Jims and Bills and Daves stamping visas through eternity in places that require a plague shot to get into, while all the J. Webster Bills get the top assignments. Anyway, I grabbed his arm, welcomed him warmly, and pointed him toward the bar.

The guests were starting to flow in now, and I stood at the door repeating my mantra: warm welcome, cool drink. About a half-hour into this routine, my sisters arrived, husbands in tow. The Jewish Pixie had a shopping bag and addressed my husband: "We (a reference to the feline sister beside her) brought you something," she said, stretching the last syllable and giving it a lilt. My husband cast a wary eye. Like a lot of professional men he is sensitive about his dignity, which, love him though I do, he has in greater abundance than striking good looks. In one motion the Pixie reached into the bag, pulled out a pot covered in a shiny substance, and set it on his head. "It's a Viking helmet! You have to wear it!" she proclaimed. Actually, it was a colander covered in aluminum foil with two large horns crafted out of the same material attached. To his credit he left it on, but I do believe he helped himself to another drink.

By nine everyone was there: the Texan, Mr. Diplomat and Mrs. Diplomat, the Southern Belle and Mr. Belle, the Blue and her spouse, the Officer-Who-Awoke-on-the-Beach, the VSYD of course, the Dutch diplomat, Mr. and Mrs. California Guy and Girl, the English Rose and her spouse (who had a thing for the cheese ball), the Japanese Flower and her spouse, the Young Military Officer and his wife, plus all the others including My Nude Neighbor. He was a Brit with one of the Hong Kong trading houses, and he had a penchant for walking around his flat in the altogether, which should not have been anyone else's business, except he never drew his bedroom drapes and his bedroom overlooked the rock garden behind the building where my husband and I sometimes walked in the evening. He was a nice enough guy of considerable means if somewhat more modest proportions.

My husband—still with helmet—began the official part of the evening by offering a welcoming toast with the aquavit. I do not remember exactly what he said (although I know he called on Leif Erikson to bless the gathering and promised an expedition later to rape and pillage Stanley Village), but I do clearly remember the look on his face when the aquavit hit bottom, producing a sharp intake of breath that left him hollow-cheeked and red-eyed. With the colander now askew, he looked like he had been hit by lightning. Twice.

The party quickly moved into high gear. We sisters moved on Mrs. Diplomat who was decked out in an orange jumpsuit—very seventies—that featured an oversize front zipper with a large circular pull. We had long wondered about Mrs. Diplomat's true nature. She seemed incredibly passive but at the same time projected an aura of being open to almost anything. I don't know what came over me, but I do remember the Pixie saying something about the zipper. In any case, my hand (all by itself) reached up and gave the large circular pull a yank. Downward. Mrs. Diplomat just stood there, proud and unencumbered by restraining garments. The Texan, who was married to the feline sister and was everywhere throughout the evening, loudly pronounced them "best in show". The other guests simply turned, focused, and then went back to their conversations. I thought she at least merited polite applause.

If we Sisters were the driving force, the Texan was Everyman. He was the opposite of his catlike spouse: loud, brash, incapable of being anywhere but center stage. He had a wicked sense of humor that often got the best of him because he was prone to blurt first and think second, especially after a couple drinks. He moved around the room with an ease that I found amazing and envied because I lacked his gift. Everyman was Everywhere. One moment he was passing verdict on Mrs. Diplomat, the next he was locked in intense negotiations with the Dutch counselor. The Dutchman was speaking Dutch, which the Texan did not, and the Texan was speaking Chinese, which the Dutchman did not, and every point was being contested and punctuated with deep draughts from their glasses until the Texan stood bolt upright, asked for silence, and proclaimed in his commanding voice that having won the consent of Her Majesty's Royal Dutch government he was pleased to announce his engagement to the Japanese Flower. He then drained his glass and kissed the Japanese Flower, who had not the slightest idea what was happening.

I joined my husband, who had watched all this, including the affair of the zipper (now returned to its normal setting), with Mr. Diplomat, who seemed not all that bothered. Cool customers, these veteran diplomats. In fact, he was far more interested in the aquavit, which he was trying—unsuccessfully—to light with his Zippo. He was explaining all this in a monologue to my husband. It reminded him of the native product of his Border State home, he said, and he asserted flammability to be the true test of fine distilled spirits. Mr. Diplomat was a good man, an excellent linguist and a very effective representative of US interests, but he lacked the political connections (and the crazy name) to go to the top of the department. As he downed his unlit shot, he changed topics waxing nostalgic about Big Red, a working girl back home who apparently made up in affability what she lacked in looks. I had the distinct impression he had never experienced her favors first hand, but she had clearly made a strong impression on the boys in his high school gym class.

His monologue was punctuated by a crash. California Girl, who was very tall and striking, had reached the point in her evening where she demonstrated her very long legs—thirty-three inches inseam, she announced—by raising her right foot and setting it on the edge of the coffee table. Twenty-nine of the thirty-three inches were clearly visible, and the Texan—apparently trying to get an angle on the missing four inches—backed into the California Guy, dividing his loaded plate between his open shirt and the floor.

My cleaning compulsion seized me, and I was in action before the echo of the crash died away. Some fire departments are not as quick to a potential disaster as I am, and I was on the scene with water, rug cleaner, and brush before California Guy could disentangle his shirt and his dinner. The Texan had taken a position behind and to my left so he would be in a better position to comment on the action. He was generous with his encouragement. California Boy and Girl and (I think) the Pixie were at work picking up pieces of salad, appetizer, and artichoke hearts, while I scrubbed away on all fours.

I cannot be sure, but I suspect it was the feline sister—I can imagine the gleam in her eye—who pointed out that California Guy's chest bore a remarkable similarity to the carpet in both stain and texture. I should never have had that second drink. The next thing I knew we were in the middle of a communal shampoo. Some worked on the rug, some worked on the California Guy, and some seemed to be working on one another. Soap bubbles floated up from the middle of the room, catching the soft light and adding to the festive air. People commented, sipped at their drinks, and nibbled at their snacks, but no one seemed to think it odd that a half-dozen or so people were sitting around an increasingly damp carpet shampooing anything they could get their hands on.

Mercifully, the amah announced that the main courses were finally ready. They were an hour and a half late, and no one seemed to mind. We adjourned to the restocked smorgasbord, filling glasses and plates, and then moved off in small groups to resume our various conversations. I noticed that the cheese ball seemed to have bits of carpet fiber stuck to it, which didn't seem to be discouraging people from trying it, but, more surprising, I could see two clear and very different sets of teeth marks in it. I remember wondering if they were bobbing for cheese balls when my back was turned. The party had settled into a zone, ebbing and flowing, marked by laughter and general good humor. We were getting our second wind.

The Blue was responsible for the next bout of silliness. The Blue was an interesting lady. Blonde in the German manner and with the cool air of a blue diamond, she was very stylish. But there was the voice. It was as if Grace Kelly opened her mouth to speak and out came Thelma Ritter. The Blue, who earlier had been trying to reopen the wine she'd brought by biting through the cork, was now insisting that any party worth its salt had people dancing on the tables, and with that she kicked off her shoes and stepped on the large square coffee table. She began to sway gracefully back and forth, moving slowly around the floral display.

The Texan immediately sensed an opportunity. One moment he was talking to the Young Military officer (YMO) and the next he was on his back slithering—no other description is possible—under the table. As The Blue moved softly to the music in her head, the Texan was emitting—again the only description possible—ooh la la sounds from beneath The Blue's feet. The coffee table, of course, was solid oak, and the only possible source of the Texan's excitement was the grain in the wood or the manufacturer's shipping marks. His well-lubricated and over-active imagination, however, continued to pump out ooh la la's until there was a sharp crash and then stillness. The Texan had tried to sit up.

The YMO and my husband grabbed the Texan by the feet and pulled him from under the table. His eyes were open, but he had a greenish tint about the gills. By the time they got him on his feet, he was near crisis. He glanced left toward the line at the bathroom, then broke right toward the balcony. It would have worked, too, except I had strung fine mesh wire between the uprights to keep our infant daughter from tossing her rattle through the bars. The YMO and my husband peeled the Texan off the wire. He had pressed so hard against it that his face was criss-crossed with little "x"s.

He looked like he had been performing an unnatural act on a waffle iron. We got him upright and into the bath off the master bedroom where he spent the rest of the evening.

The silliness seemed to ease after that, but the laughter and good humor continued unabated. It was almost three when couples started to say their thank yous. The Officer-Who-Awoke-On-The-Beach offered to give the VSYD a ride home. I thought this was very odd because they lived on opposite sides of the island and, to the best of my knowledge, neither one had a car. My sisters were among the last to go. We all policed up the Texan. I do not remember much after that, but the Pixie insists to this day that I called her once she got home and had her come back and help put my husband to bed. I am not sure I believe it, but I cannot dispute it either.

* * *

By Monday morning the story of the party was all over and its legend grew with each telling. To this day you can bring a wry smile to the lips of more than a few senior officers when you mention Leif Erikson Day. Some of what you may hear is not true, but I can tell you what is. We had a good time. We all felt better afterward, even if our heads throbbed. And on Monday, the diplomats returned to the front rooms and the well-lighted offices in the halls of power where they represented US interests most effectively; the spies, too, returned to work in the side streets and the dark places where they hunt those who harbor harm to Americans.

Thanksgiving Memories

My favorite holiday memory was the Thanksgiving of my daughter's senior year in high school. I decided that we should have a big Thanksgiving dinner and invited twenty-four friends to come for dinner. It would be a lot of fun because there were usually only the three of us for holiday celebrations. I wanted our daughter to take a special holiday memory with her when she went off to college. When I was a child, we'd always had huge family celebrations at Thanksgiving but because we were overseas now, we had to become each others' extended families. I borrowed two round table tops from a local Chinese restaurant so that we could all be seated. Before dinner, some of my friends came to help out. I remember that Ruth had made some special Swedish cookies for dessert, but they never made the dessert table. We ate them as we prepared the dinner.

My daughter just loved all the hustle and bustle and the wonderful smells that came from our kitchen. It was going to be a truly marvelous holiday. I hired extra maids to help serve, and at 3 P.M., we all gathered for the feast. We ate and ate and ate some more. Afterward, people stretched out on our sofas, beds, floors for a little snooze before we had dessert. It was a magical day and we had a wonderful time recalling our favorite holidays dinners from childhood or ones that we had spent overseas. I was so excited that I found that I did not feel melancholy about not being home for the holidays. One man had brought sauerkraut to eat with the turkey, an old Baltimore tradition, he said. It sounds terrible, but it really was quite tasty. Even today, I cannot see sauerkraut without remembering this special day.

That evening, after everyone had left and we had finished cleaning up, I decided to call my mother to tell her about the special memory that we had made for our daughter. My mother had made so many special memories for my sister and me and I just wanted her to know that I remembered and was grateful to her for all the love and work she had put into those special Thanksgiving dinners. It would be morning for her and she would just be waking up. I had never called my mother on Thanksgiving—we always called her at Christmas or New Year's, but this year I just needed to talk with her and tell her that I loved her.

I still cannot believe how lucky I was to have called her that day, because one week later to the day, she was dead. If I had waited until Christmas, I never would have been able to tell her all these things or share the special memory we had made for her granddaughter so many thousands of miles away from home. If I feel the need to talk with someone, I take the time to call because we never know . . .

Chapter VII

SEE SPOT RUN
SEE SPOT RUN AND SLITHER
SEE SPOT RUN AND SLITHER AND EAT A SNAKE

All families should have pets. They come in all sizes and shapes. Overseas they come in many more varieties than the old familiar dog back home. A snake at a cocktail party? A scorpion in the bathtub? A monkey at a dinner party?

You must be kidding! At some posts, the roaches were so large that the children would race them.

The Roaches Wore Wedding Dresses

Addis Ababa was full of stray dogs. Puppies were everywhere and the Ethiopians were very cruel to them. I would pick up two or three puppies every week and take them to the Embassy, wash them up, tie blue ribbons around their necks (even though they were all female), and pass them off to embassy officers. Months later, when their "male" puppies gave birth, they would come to me and let me know the "the puppy you gave me was a girl, did you know?" I just smiled.

Bugs are always a problem in third-world countries. Ethiopians have flies living on their faces and think nothing of it, even though it is not difficult to get rid of the flies with a swat. No one there kills them, so they are caught unaware when swatted. The roaches are a different story. They are usually the size of a roller skate and have very hard shells, and no one ever told me they fly. They do. A can of bug spray does nothing to them, and they walk around with enough bug foam that they look like a small bride on her wedding day with a ten-foot train of white.

Now, Manila had its share of wedding-dress roaches that were so large we could hear them walking on the marble floors. We also had geckos (small lizards) hanging upside-down from the ceilings, and I remember my first night there. I could not sleep for fear one would lose his suction cups and drop down in the bed. They were particularly thick around light fixtures on the outside of the house, and once a gecko dropped down the front of my evening dress as I was going in my front door. That sucker got a run for his money! Cocktail party conversation inevitably got around to a gecko story at some point in the evening. We had them fall on cards at bridge games and in the soup at a dinner party with the guests running off into the next room in fright.

Rome had its incidents also. I remember one day going to the central market to shop with a friend. We encountered a wealthy Italian woman in her fur coat, Gucci everything else, including boots. She was there supervising her maid, who was doing the actual shopping. A chicken that had been hanging upside-down on one of the overhead lines, along with hundreds of other live chickens and rabbits, fell on her bouffant hairdo feet first! The chicken dug its claws into her hair and began to squawk and poop, squawk and poop—everywhere—her hair, her coat, her purse—the woman was turning white from it. She was screaming "ayuto, ayuto" (help) and jumping around. The more she screamed, the more the chicken pooped and held on to her hair. By then all the other chickens were screeching and the din was unbearable. Eventually, the chicken was cut free, but not before the lady had lost hair and a lot of her Gucci wardrobe.

The Cobra Who Came to Dinner

It was our first tour in Bangkok and we were having a dinner party. Just before the guests were due to arrive, we found a King Cobra snake curled up in the bottom of one of our end tables, a bamboo fish basket with a glass top on it. We had geese in the yard to keep the snakes under control so we brought in the geese to get the Cobra. The geese were hissing, the children were screaming, the snake was moving around the room, and the guests were arriving. All ended successfully when the gardener appeared with a bamboo pole, caught the snake, and brought him out into the yard. We made martinis and remarked on the hazards of living in Southeast Asia. Another normal day.

But My Dog Doesn't Bite!

After months of electrical outages in our apartment, the power company came to install an additional line to increase the voltage. As the crew prepared to leave, I was informed that they would be disconnecting the old box and the embassy would have to come out and connect the new one. I told them this was impossible at five o'clock in the afternoon on a Friday. That was not their problem. I ran to call the embassy but could reach no one. I ran back to tell the electrician that all the food in the freezer would be ruined, to say nothing of no stove and no lights. Mr. Pompous stood dead in his tracks when he saw Buster Bambino, our sweet boxer, come into the room. He was petrified and demanded that I tie the dog up. I told him he need not worry, the dog did not bite "Unless Madame tells him to!" added my little cherub cook, who was right behind Buster. The man hastily agreed to leave things as they were until the following week, when he would send someone out to disconnect the line. Cook gave Buster more treats than usual that evening, and one very passive Buster took to his lounging corner again, as usual.

These Boots Were Made for Stomping

After repeated requests to the Government Services Office (GSO) for an exterminator to get rid of those thumb-sized flying roaches in our apartment in our new post in Southeast Asia, I sent in yet another request with an option: "Please send exterminator, or one pair of combat boots to stomp out gargantuan roaches!"

That day, the GSO who lived above me called out laughing from the balcony to let me know he had received my note. He became hysterical, however, when I pranced out in a short skirt sporting my husband's black, marine-issue combat boots. I thanked him as I jumped around showing him how well they worked. The exterminator with the chemicals showed up the next day.

Jalle

A baby cheetah whose mother had died was offered to us by a friend, a Kurdish Iraqi diplomat who had taken the other cub. After learning what the responsibilities would be in nurturing and planning for its future, with the children cheerleading, we agreed we would care for this noble and demanding creature. Unfortunately, before the spotted feline with permanent lamenting black tears streaming from its eyes could be moved to our compound, it died of rickets, as is very common among cheetah cubs. How presumptuous it seems now that we thought we could somehow take possession and do justice by this wild creature with whom we could have no common ground. To train him in the knowledge of our gods would be to extinguish the fire of his very being.

We were all saddened by the cheetah's death and in response let it be known to a few friends that we would be interested in getting a dog. The children very much wanted a pet. Before long another friend, a French diplomat, arrived with a German Shepherd puppy who became known as Jalle, "comrade," in Somali. We kept his name quiet. With the strong Soviet political influence and the Islamic view of a dog as an unclean animal, we were bantering with a culpable offense to religion and state. Jalle thrived for about a year and a half, until one day we found him unable to move and listless. There were no vets in Somalia, but there was a veterinarian school of animal husbandry in the outskirts of Mogadishu, which I brought him to with the reluctant aid of my servant. I knew he was dying and was probably poisoned and was astounded by the animal practitioner's advice that I brush his teeth with a particular solution. He died at home within three hours and was buried in the garden under a row of red hibiscus.

Dinner Entertainment

Whenever I think of exotic pets, I remember my friend's monkey in Bangkok. I guess by now everyone who has watched nature shows on television knows that monkeys have terrible habits and should never be raised as pets. However, back in the sixties, we were not so knowledgeable and thought that monkeys were just adorable. My attitude changed during our tour in Bangkok, after I met my friend's monkey, which she had purchased at the Sunday Market. This monkey was nasty and the only person who liked it was my friend. Her maids wanted her to get rid of it because the monkey would urinate all over the house whenever she was not at home. Somehow he knew that he had to keep Madame happy or he would be looking for a new home. Whenever she was around, he was on his best behavior. This changed one evening when my friend hosted a dinner party. After we all were seated at the table, the monkey proceeded to jump up on the buffet and began to masturbate. Those of us who could see him tried to look elsewhere and pretend that it was not happening, but the little devil added some sounds that were definitely orgasmic. By now, even the people who were seated with their backs to the monkey had figured out what was going on. The hostess kept talking louder and louder and tried to keep up some semblance of conversation as if none of this were happening. Finally the monkey climaxed, or whatever monkeys do, and we all continued on as if nothing had happened. It was a memorable evening.

Charlie

For Chinese New Year in the Philippines, we were given a gift of two live capons. I had the maids kill one of the roosters, and we made chicken soup. Our daughter refused to eat at home that night because she thought chicken soup came in cans and they didn't use live chickens for it. By the time we got around to thinking of killing the second chicken, he had been named Charlie by our daughter and he was her pet. So Charlie began his life with us in Manila. He was a beautiful red rooster who used to roost in the banyan tree in the backyard to survey his domain. He loved to terrorize our dog, and whenever the dog entered the backyard, Charlie would swoop down and peck his back. The dog was not the smartest and kept going back for morc. Wc had a Siamese cat to add to the menagerie. She was a haughty cat and loved the screened porch. One day the cat sat with her nose pressed to the screen. Suddenly Charlie swooped down and pecked her nose. I had never seen a cat fly before, but she was airborne and flew straight back six feet. She never pressed her nose on the screen again.

Charlie became a beloved pet of the family after he saved us from a burglar. One night, when my husband was on one of his constant TDYs, the maids woke me to say that someone had tried to break into the house. They had been awakened by Charlie clucking and carrying on. They knew that it was unusual for Charlie to be awake, so they got up to see what was wrong. When they turned on the light in the hallway, they found that the door had been forced open and only the chain lock was holding it intact. They heard a person flee, obviously scared off by Charlie. The police did not find the burglar, but Charlie was the Neighborhood Watch Rooster from then on. For the rest of our tour he had our utmost respect and lived a happy life in the banyan tree. We gave him to another couple when we left Manila, and he continued on his job.

Rome, The City of Cats

One afternoon in Rome, I was sitting on the curb outside our apartment waiting for the school bus when this cute little gray kitten showed up out of nowhere. Sucker! I scurried off to get a bowl of milk and the poor thing moved in with us. The *portiera*, the lady manager of the apartment building, did not like seeing me with this kitten. But too bad; American lady pay rent, American lady have kitten. We named her Senora Gatta, Mrs. Kitten. One day I noticed that she was gaining weight at a rapid rate. She kept getting fatter and fatter, and I finally figured out she was expecting. This cat was really quite smart—she lived outside in the cat house especially designed for her. She would come in the apartment building, up to our second-story apartment, and meow to get in and visit for a few hours. One day she meowed, I opened the door, and she flew into the apartment with something in her mouth and made herself comfortable. It was a tiny baby kitten, which she deposited under my daughter's bed. Senora Gatta meowed to get out again and returned in a few minutes with another kitten. On the third try, I went downstairs to the cat house and discovered seven more kittens. I took the ones from under the bed and redeposited them in the downstairs home. Within fifteen minutes she was back at the door with a kitten in her mouth. She finally won and they all moved in to my daughter's room until they were old enough to be given to friends.

Oh Rats!

We had been putting sand-filled tubes under the entrances of the house at night to keep out the *haboob* (sand storm) dust, but each morning some bags had been chewed through and gifts were left by visiting rats. I lived in mortal terror that a rat—and they were all rabid, we were told—would bite my toddler. Late one evening, I heard the front door open, but my husband did not come into the bedroom to tell me he was home. As I sat up to listen for him, I came face to face with a "cute" brown rat peeking out from behind the curtains. After slamming the baby's door shut, I ran out of the house screaming. After calming me down, the guard and my husband went in search of the rat, who had jumped into the golf bag at the end of the hall. As the guard tried to smash him in the bag with a golf club, the rat leapt out over my husband's shoulder. Both men chased the rat out of the house. The guard repeatedly tried to kill it with a three wood while my husband wielded the five iron. With a swift blow, the guard smashed the vermin's head and pitched the body into the gutter outside the gate. "Tell Madam he is finished," beamed the guard as he returned the soiled club to the bag of a "soon-to-be-retired golfer."

Chapter VIII

CONTRACT WIVES

Wives were used as contract employees, hired in the field to fill needed jobs without having to use staff employees assigned by Washington. This meant that management could then fill most of the slots with operational officers and still maintain the personnel ceiling mandated for each station. By using contract wives, the station could save money.

In the early years, contract wives served as slave labor. Many of them had worked for the agency in Washington, but in the days before "tandem couples," a transfer to the field by the officer meant that the spouse must automatically resign from staff employment in Washington and follow her husband to his assigned post. Quite often the wives were reports officers, finance officers, technical and communications specialists that could be hired at a fraction of their former pay grades. There were no evaluations of performance for contract wives in the field, no record of their employment. No references for future employment were kept. Thus, subsequent potential employers could not check on a contract wife's work assignments overseas. There appeared to be huge gaps in her employment history. Often, the contract wife could not tell anyone outside the station that she was working. This made it interesting with friends on the

"Outside." Where did she go each day? She couldn't even give out her office telephone number to friends and children. For many years, these rules were followed. Then the natives got restless. Many wives refused contract employment and lobbied instead for career contract employment tracks. This goal has not been reached, but some improvements have been achieved.

The biggest shock for most contract wives was the knowledge that they could not just return to the States and a job at headquarters. They had to apply like anyone off the street. It takes approximately twelve months for an applicant to process and be hired for employment. Since operation officers were usually off on another assignment in a short time, it was impossible for these women to have a career either in or outside the agency.

Contract wives brought a wealth of knowledge to each new assignment. They made major contributions wherever they went and contributed to many of CIA's operational successes.

Hearts, Minds, and Orange Soda

The prisoner was arriving from Quang Nai City on the Air America Beechcraft airplane that was just coming in over Monkey Mountain; Danang was experiencing a monsoon that day. I was a "contract wife" working at our CIA office in Danang. The starched pale pink embroidered dress belonged in Georgetown and not in I Corps, Vietnam, but who cares when you are twenty-four years old and trying to look civilized in this jungle of despair? I had never seen the Viet Cong before, or at least not one that I knew to be Viet Cong. Sure, they were probably in every noodle shop but they did not look any different from all the other Vietnamese. I was about to meet one face to face.

The pilot came to a quick stop at the Air America shack. These guys flew in any kind of weather. I was out there to meet the courier flight from Saigon to pick up the classified pouch. The prisoner was going to be transferred here to the courier plane for his trip to the Interrogation Center in Saigon. As the pilot leaped down and stuck his head back into the plane, a feeling of fear came over me. How would I handle this? Out came two skinny handcuffed wrists followed by a tiny body in a black pajama uniform. Eyes wide with fear and hatred. So were mine. We had a two hour wait, and I was determined to approach it with caution. There was a tumble-down table with three benches around it near the tarmac. Fanta orange soda and tons of BaMeBa, the local beer, were in a cooler courtesy of our local Air America representative. Sit and pretend that this is a social occasion, I told myself. Good luck! We sat there. No words could be exchanged because no common language existed between us, or so we thought. I lifted the Fanta bottle, nodded my head, and he nodded.

Manipulating the handcuffs, he was able to pick up the soda and drain it. I took out my pack of Benson and Hedges, a sophisticated box of gold and brown and white, the way they used to make them. Elegant packaging when it was considered elegant to smoke. I offered him one. He took it clumsily, and I lit it for him. And so we sat . . . smiled . . . smoked . . . and drank Fanta. The loud drone of the C-46 gray courier plane soon filled the air with dread. The prisoner looked up. I looked up. It arrived, unloaded its cargo of pigs and bulgar wheat. The escort from Saigon gave the prisoner a Dramamine pill for the flight. They tended to throw up and it was going to be a bumpy ride, he informed us. He reluctantly swallowed the pill, not sure if cyanide poisoning might be worse than his unknown fate. The prisoner was then lifted onto the plane and belted into one of the jump seats in the rear. This guy was dangerous. He had been picked up at night in a village where he did not belong, recruiting the male villagers to join him in the North for training with the promise of a better life for this village in the future. One of them had informed on him. So now here he was, off to a jail cell and interrogation. I doubted he would see the Saigon I knew—the city of great French crepe suzettes and Soup Chinoise, of sidewalk cafes and sultry gin and tonic afternoons at the Cerque Sportif, of big steaks at the Rex Hotel, and cold martinis on the top of the Caravelle Hotel. Off he went—over Marble Mountain and into a world I could not envision.

Six months later, I was driving my Chevrolet Corvair down the main street of Danang along the river. I had an envelope of secret cables to take over to the "White Elephant," the navy SOG office. No more pink starched dress; now khaki pants, sleeveless shirt, and sandals. The glove compartment held a gun that I had learned to fire. Our guys at the White Elephant knew I was coming because we always called first when we roamed around town transporting classified information. What they did not realize was that there was a demonstration going on downtown. As I approached the center of town, there was a large crowd in front of me marching slowly down the street. They were pushing two wheelchairs with effigies in them, one with a "Taylor Go Home" (Maxwell Taylor was the American ambassador at this time) and one with "Down with Huong" (Huong was the president of the Republic of Vietnam). The crowd grew larger. The masses of people kept coming. Closer and closer. What to do? Lock the doors but don't open the glove compartment yet. Sit and wait. They stopped in front of the car. A group pressed their noses to the window. They had been turning over cars and burning them for weeks. Buddhists and Catholics burning each other's villages. But never an American. Visions of those charred automobiles danced in my head and they were not like sugar plums. These people were South Vietnamese; surely they would not do me any harm. I was here to help them. I waited. They paraded past. They kept looking in the windows and shouting but they kept on marching by. The longest fifteen minutes of my life, and I sure did not want this to be my fifteen minutes of fame. They kept looking in the windows and shouting but kept on marching by. I drove off as they disappeared from sight.

Seven months into our tour in Danang, and by now we were known in the city and greeted at every turn. The pink starched dress long packed away and the innocent little girl was gone. Memories overcome me: Driving a jeep and off to My Khe Beach at lunch time during siesta for a few rays of sun, a weapon on the front seat if I need it. A trip over Aivan Pass to enjoy the scenery on a slow Sunday afternoon, making sure to get back before dusk as this was Viet Cong territory at night. A long evening spent at the Doom Club at the Danang Air Force Base putting pencil to paper to argue about successful points of the Strategic Hamlet Pacification Program. Staring gratefully at the wing of the Air America plane where it had taken a bullet while flying low over the hills during a landing at Tam Ky. Glad it was the wing and not the engine. Damn, why couldn't we win this war!

There was a rally on the steps of the Danang City Hall that day and I walked over with our translator, Ky, to see what was going on. Several people in the crowd greeted me. There was a respectable and nicely dressed young man addressing the crowd over a loud speaker. Ky told me what he said. The young man had been taken prisoner by the South Vietnamese several months earlier. A kind American lady had given him a soda and American cigarettes when he had stopped in Danang. He had been sent to Saigon for interrogation and now he was working for the South Vietnamese government, identifying and eliminating infiltrators in the villages of I Corps. He thanked the Americans, and particularly the American lady for showing him so much kindness.

Maybe it is time to haul out the old starched pink embroidered dress and have a look at it to bring back the human side of that horrible war.

A Lost Opportunity

I was a "contract wife." In essence, I was cheap labor. I had joined the agency after graduation from college. My husband joined a year later. He went into the Junior Officer Trainee (JOT) Program later known as the Career Trainee (CT) Program. I wanted to apply to this program but was told I could not because wives were not allowed; single females only. (This sexist policy was later changed.) In the sixties, when an individual was assigned overseas, his spouse, if she was a staff employee, had to resign at headquarters in order to accompany her husband. If there was a need for her services at the station, she would then be put on the station payroll and paid by the hour when working. The pay was close to minimum wage, but it beat staying home and watching the maid clean the castle.

I was assigned to work at the Interrogation Center (IC) in a town in Southeast Asia. It was a jail. Believe me, it wasn't all guns and roses in that joint either. The prisoners were kept in cells on the main level and the administrative "offices" were on the top floor. The view from my office window was the central courtyard where the prisoners were taken out for an "airing" twice a day. Lunch was downstairs in the kitchen. Coagulated blood soup was the usual fare and once in awhile we got a chicken that was split into enough pieces to feed both the prisoners and the staff. The facility was funded by the station and hence, the American advisors at the IC were treated like manna from heaven. Actually, we were manna from heaven. Our reasons for being there and doing this were valid. This was a country suffering from a communist insurgency. Communists were infiltrating into the villages all over the country. A cadre of loyalists were reporting this daily. My duty was to take these reports, attempt to discover the correct names, and locate the communists. We set up a file system to help identify suspects. The next step in the process was for the police or military to capture these individuals and bring them down to the big city for interrogation at our center. During the interrogation the prisoner was encouraged to identify fellow villagers sympathetic to the communist cause and key leaders from China who were active in the area. It was a big day when we captured a prisoner who had been to China. One day we picked up a husband-and-wife team trained in China, who had been active in the jungle for years. They arrived at the center on Monday morning and she had a baby five days later. I supplied her with my son's clothes as she had nothing and was living in a cell. Now, these cells were not Hilton hotel rooms. They were six feet by five feet with a concrete slab for a bed and a hole in the ground for a toilet. There was a small vent at the top for a bit of the humid, hot tropical heat to enter.

My job at the IC was to make sure the place ran smoothly and to win "hearts and minds." I carried the payroll over once a month, which won a lot of hearts and minds. I spent endless hours each day trying to understand the English translations of the reports, screen the reports for any tidbits of "real intelligence," and report any significant information to the case officer. My duties included daily interaction with the staff of translators, interrogators, guards, and high-level senior staff. I was frequently the only American out there for weeks on end; the one case officer assigned to the IC was more interested in the bars downtown. He felt I was responsible enough to know which bar he was in, in case there was a need to contact him. I was.

I did my job well. I took it seriously and I liked it. The case officer who knew all the bars in town had returned to the States and was not replaced. I took over the work completely. Over the years, I had developed a good professional relationship with the general who was our liaison point of contact. We ate together, socialized together, anguished over the prisoners together, went through weddings, births, promotions, automobile accidents, hirings and firings of staff together. In short, we knew each other well. We had some successes, filed some fine reports, captured and successfully interrogated hundreds of prisoners. I had been there almost five years. It was time to leave.

The ultimate success for a case officer is to recruit a high-level source. The liaison general was a high-level source. He knew what was going on in the top levels of the government. This had been proven to me, and reported by me and the station knew it. I wanted to recruit him. I felt he was recruitable. He lived way above his means. His children were being educated overseas. His house was a mansion. He drove a Mercedes Benz. He ate in the best restaurants. He had a lot of debts. His salary was his only visible means of support, and he liked the good life. He liked Americans and liked me. I brought the subject of recruitment up to my immediate superior at the station. It would be a feather in his cap even if he had not been directly involved. He was happy to listen and suggested we send a cable back to headquarters. The chief of station (COS) was on home leave and the deputy chief of station (DCOS) laughed and said they would never approve it at headquarters. However, he felt obliged to send the recruitment proposal back to Washington. The case officer in charge of the desk at Langley happened to be the same "bar hopper" who had worked with me earlier in our tour. A cable came back: *"Are we to assume that a contract wife is going to attempt this recruitment?"* I sent a cable back that simply said *"Yes!"* Headquarters, with some trepidation, came back and said "Try it if the DCOS concurs." Damn. A local roadblock.

This DCOS had been having personal problems and I knew him well—he was in the throes of a messy divorce. He couldn't type and he needed to write to his lawyer about the sordid details of his separation. Earlier that year, he had asked me to type his personal correspondence to his attorney because I was discreet and could type it at a remote site. I did this and told no one. It was a wonderful story for one of the supermarket checkout rags. Who cares, it goes on all the time. I promptly filed it away and forgot about it.

The DCOS called me into his office and said that he did not agree with the recruitment attempt, but it had gotten some press at headquarters and he told me that I should meet the general just days prior to my departure. I was told to simply elicit enough information from him to find out if he was recruitable but I was not to recruit him. I suggested that maybe we could try that all around the world and give the KGB a good laugh.

"I know he is recruitable," I told him.

"How do you know this? If you do know this, you must be sleeping with him!" After I took myself off the ceiling, I calmed down. I did not want to ruin my husband's career by telling him what I really thought. So I agreed.

For a moment before my meeting with the general, I thought, the hell with it. I'll just recruit him anyway. My husband agreed. But then I thought of all our years with this organization and I decided not to risk it.

The big lunch came. We talked about my departure and how they were going to miss me at the IC. We were about to finish up, and I said, "If there is anything I can do for you before I leave, please let me know." He paused, shuddered, and said "What can you do for me?" The moment of truth. I paused, shuddered, and said "I wish I knew." We parted company that day, both pensive and confused.

That general went on to get three more stars, assumed numerous high level positions in the government, and could have been a top-level source of intelligence information. But he was never recruited.

A lost opportunity, and all because I was a contract wife.

From the Ground Up

It was a warm June day in Manila, where my son and I were living at the time. I was a "Saigon wife," which meant my husband was in Vietnam and we were in a safe haven in the Philippines. The war was winding down and my husband's tour ended. After many years of a rocky marriage, we decided to separate. The separated tour made us realize that there was no future for our relationship. After making that decision, I realized that I had to make a plan for my future. What could I do? I had been working as a contract wife, but that was the only practical work experience I had had. I had married right out of college—my husband was already an officer at the agency—so we had started our gypsy life right away. I had never thought about a career, but I realized now that if I was going to take care of my son and myself, I would have to think about one. Considering my only practical experience had been working as a contract wife, I decided to join the agency. Now in the mid-seventies, this was not an easy task, but I was determined. I contacted an attorney in Maryland, who arranged for our divorce in Santo Domingo. My husband agreed to the divorce and signed the legal separation agreement.

My son and I left Manila and flew to Miami, and from there to Santo Domingo where, three days later, I was free. My parents thought that I would return to New York and live near them, but I knew that I could not go home again, plus I had already arranged for all of our household effects to be shipped to Washington. Fortunately, a friend had called me and told me that I could stay with her while I applied for a job and rented an apartment. I left my son with my parents and headed down to Washington. Within a week, I was working for the DEA (Drug Enforcement Administration) and had rented an apartment, bought a car and, more importantly, I had applied to the agency for a position. I could not type and before I could get a job with DEA, I had to pass a typing test! My friend who was helping me get the job with DEA was determined that I would learn to type in five easy lessons. She signed me up with a secretarial school and I had a crash course in typing. It took me about eight typing tests, but I finally passed. I was hired as a GS 4, Step 1, and would be earning $8,000, per year. It is a good thing that I was young or I would have been daunted by the fact that we had gone from an income of around $25,000 per year to $8,000 but when one is young and determined, anything is possible. By that September, my son and I were settled into our new life in Virginia.

I worked at DEA for six months before I cleared all the hurdles of security clearances, etc., to gain employment at the agency. I started as a clerk typist and quickly decided that this was not where I wanted to be. Computers had just started to come into the work place, so I took all the computer courses I could and learned programming and as much about computers as I possibly could. Eventually I worked my way up to be chief of training for computers. I created a branch to support the officers who were using this new automation at headquarters. I manage a staff of 145 people today.

It wasn't an easy climb, but I did it. Imagine what more women could have done if somehow the agency had made arrangements for all who worked as contract wives to come in at staff levels when they returned from overseas.

Honey, I'll Be Late

I was a contract wife working for the chief of support at the station. One of our responsibilities was the "care and feeding of safe houses." A "safe house" was a domicile that was usually rented in a fictitious name and maintained for the sole purpose of meeting operational assets in a controlled or "safe" environment. It was frequently off the beaten path and allowed for privacy when meeting agents who dared not be seen with you in public. Safe houses came in all shapes and sizes—large villas where a defector may have lived for an extended period of time, or as usually was the case, one-bedroom apartments where meetings took place. In most stations there were several safe houses, because different case officers frequently had a need for a safe house at the same time or on the same day. Consequently, a schedule was kept to avoid any security problems. Asset A should not come face to face with Asset B, particularly if they might recognize each other.

I was in charge of the safe house scheduling, keys, cleaning, and re-stocking. Alcohol and snacks were the bill of fare in all safe houses. I knew which case officer was using which safe house, but I did not know who they were meeting. I had to re-stock each safe house on a regular basis. When one was not in use, I would bring in the usual supplies of bourbon, scotch, gin, and vodka with mixers and nuts. I would check to see that the place was clean, towels replenished, ice cubes made, and trash emptied. There was little else to do.

Upon my visit to a particular safe house one afternoon, I replenished the bar and noticed that there was a bottle of Pernod. I had not put it there. I simply brushed it off. I went back to the office and checked that this particular safe house had been used frequently, so I figured there was some agent who liked Pernod.

Two weeks later I returned again. The Pernod was still there, although less of it. The bedroom was in slight disarray and had obviously been used. Oh well, they worked long hours and deserved a nap once in a while. I returned to the office and checked the schedule again. Nothing strange—just the usual suspects.

The third visit added to the mystery. A new bottle of Pernod, a rumpled bed, and a long black hair in the bathroom sink. I was getting more and more curious. The chief of station stopped in my office that morning, unaware that I was in charge of safe houses. He heard me casually mention that I had to go to the PX that day and asked me if I would buy him a bottle of Pernod. Chiefs of station are right up there next to God so I said yes. I curiously checked the schedule at that safe house and discovered that our COS had several agent meetings a week in it. He had his own set of keys to safe houses. Hmmm.

It was not until six months later that the mystery was solved. We were all at a cocktail party at the chief of station's home. His secretary, a tall, good-looking, black-haired beauty of twenty-four arrived and placed her drink order. "Pernod, please."

We continued to socialize for the appropriate amount of time, but his secretary left early. The rest of us left at the same time, including the COS, who departed with us. He turned to his wife as we were all leaving and said, "I've got to go out, honey. I'll be late. I have an agent meeting." You never know who is listening when you have a contract wife in the room!

Chapter IX

PINK SLIPS AND OTHER DIRTY LAUNDRY

The "Halloween Massacre" in October 1977 was one of the darkest moments in CIA history. The Director of CIA, by law, has the indiscriminate right to hire and fire. And fire he did. Many people believe that CIA has never recovered from this action.

The Halloween Massacre

October 1977 was one of the saddest and most debilitating periods in the history of the CIA, and particularly the Directorate of Operations (DO). Admiral Stansfield Turner was appointed by President Carter as director of the CIA (DCI). Turner orchestrated the forced retirement or firing of several hundred officers within the DO. Many people believe that the DO has never full recovered from this action, which is now remembered as the "Halloween Massacre" because it happened on All Saint's Day.

My husband, Bill, and I were stationed in California at the time of the firings. He had served with the agency for fifteen years, including overseas for seven years in Vietnam and Thailand and one year in Europe. He had entered the agency through the Junior Officers Program (JOT), and although he was not considered a "rising star" in the hallowed halls of Langley, he had risen steadily through the ranks and had strong fitness reports and promotions regularly until we got to Europe. We had a bad experience in Europe. The station had no work available for me although I had been working in Langley as a "staffer" and had been a contract employee in Asia. I felt that my career was secondary to my husband's, so I packed up and we were off again.

The tour was a disaster. There were Soviets and Chinese all over the city and we had made efforts to meet them. We entertained them frequently. I recall dining at the home of one of the KGB officers—they had a small apartment in the city and had invited us to dinner. This was considered a coup in most stations. They were so excited to entertain us that they had disassembled their entire bedroom and stored the furniture so that they could set up a table and chairs and we could all sit around the table together!

My husband had professional and personal disagreements with the COS and the DCOS—different philosophies about what his assignment was all about. We talked with each other and Washington, and it was mutually agreed that it would be wiser to return to the United States short of tour. Nothing would be gained by staying, so we were assigned to Washington. Obviously a very poor fitness report accompanied his return to headquarters and he was ranked near the bottom of his grade group in that promotion cycle. From 1974-1977, he worked his way back up in the rankings and had been nominated for promotion in 1977 when the massacre happened. The "selection out" process by Admiral Turner was based on an individual's rankings within his grade group for the previous five years. Bill was caught up in the firings because of the 1974-1975 experiences.

It was a very painful experience to see my husband fired from an organization that he had faithfully served for fifteen years. Until this time, the CIA and particularly the DO had prided itself on the loyalty and "esprit de corps" of its employees. This, after all, was not a nine-to-five job! Many of the officers had served in Vietnam and other areas of Southeast Asia and truly believed they were in the forefront of "stemming the tide of Red aggression." Most of the DO officers who "got the ax" as well as those who did not, considered the firings a betrayal of that loyalty.

November 1, 1977. We were sitting in California and my husband had just been fired. My neck muscles tightened as a trap door opened under my feet. My mother had retired from teaching and had just come to live with us. Bill's nephew came to live with us after his parents' sudden deaths the year before. We had an eleven-year-old son. We had to find a way to eat. Those who had received dismissal notices were told that they would have to be gone from the agency within five months! That gave us until April 1, 1978, ironically—April Fool's Day.

So Bill started to look for a job in California while

still working for the base. There was not a large market for former spies in the Los Angeles basin, particularly for those in their mid-forties. He sent out about 300 resumes and did not receive one positive response. Somehow his skills did not mesh with the demands of private industry, and being middle-aged did not help either. The CIA is not part of the Civil Service System and thus we could not transfer to another US government agency. I knew that I was going to have to find a job to help out and had the same problem with a resume. I could certainly assess potential assets, but I had never learned to type! That was the more marketable skill for a female returning to the job market in the seventies. I took a course and learned typing and shorthand and I was ready.

In the spring of 1978, just before Bill would be required to leave the agency, his boss in California asked headquarters in Langley to extend Bill in California until August 1978 because the base was short of personnel and needed Bill's skills and expertise to get the job done. Headquarters agreed, and so we received a reprieve until August 1978. Guess this made sense to someone, but not to me.

As I relate this, I cannot help but think of the humorous side of this dilemma. My husband was fired for incompetence but he was still working because he was competent.

By April 1978, all those who had received "pink slips" (so named because of the color of the notification memo) were gone except for Bill and a few others. In June 1978, the office in California received a request from headquarters asking the base to look for new recruits to join the CIA and the DO (Operations Directorate) in particular. Not surprisingly, the DO was now short of case officers because of the firings nine months earlier! When Bill came home and told me this, I sat and stared in utter amazement at this insanity. Here he was being asked to go out and find his own replacement. In August 1978, we moved back to Washington and I began to look for a job. I fully expected that Bill would soon be gone from the agency because the "pink slip" said so. Wrong. Bill believed that his firing was directly related to his one unfortunate year in Europe and he knew that the CIA Inspector General's (IG) office had done an investigation of the European station where Bill had served. This occurred shortly after our departure from the station and had resulted in the short-of-tour transfers of the top station management. Could there be "something rotten in Denmark"?

Bill believed that there was fault on both sides and that surely these transfers reinforced his belief. He certainly did not deserve to be fired because of his "whistle blowing," did he? The IG office agreed to review Bill's case, and he continued to work at headquarters. There were numerous job openings posted on the bulletin board resulting from the previous year's massacre. Bill applied for several of these jobs. He was initially told that he qualified for them, and senior management actually wanted to hire him for these positions. But he could not be hired because he had been fired and thus was not eligible anymore! Finally Bill's efforts to stay with the CIA, an organization he truly respected and loved, ended on December 7, 1978. Merry Christmas! Admiral Turner had won. His firings were based on the administration's desire to trim back the ranks of the clandestine service, which had swelled during the Vietnam War. A noble cause but ill-fated. The mid-level ranks of the DO, the directorate's case officer muscle, were gutted and have never recovered. Critically important experience and knowledge were gone. My husband was too.

I am happy to report that this story has a happy ending, although it took some time and a lot of money to get there. Bill took several jobs just to put food on the table—sales, security companies, and personnel search firms. None of them was satisfying financially or intellectually but he did them. He longed to return to the agency. At times, I wondered why he cared so much, but he always maintained his dignity and refused to blame the agency as a whole. He never spoke ill of his "beloved" and said that the actions of a few did not demean the organization as a whole. I will always admire him for this. Our friends remained our friends and many of them contributed to a legal fund set up for us by a former case officer, editor, and friend. They believed in him and he believed in himself. I got a job in private industry, using my typing skills as an entree into the corporate world. We ate and we believed that we could right this wrong.

When Bill left that fateful December day, he contacted a wonderful man, a lawyer who worked in Washington and had previously represented Bill Colby, the former director of the CIA, when Colby testified before Congress. My husband had taken copious notes of all that occurred during the "pink slip" process. He told Mitch (our new legal counsel) that he felt he had been wronged by the firing. He told him of his four years in the Marine Corps, where he fought in the Korean War and his combined total of nineteen years of government service. It appeared, according to Bill, that most of the fired employees were over forty years of age and perhaps there might be age discrimination involved.

Mitch agreed to accept our case. You cannot sue the United States Government or the CIA unless they let you. Our suit (and I call it ours because I cared as much as Bill did) was based on age discrimination—92% of those fired were over the age of forty. That violates a person's civil rights. However, the National Security Act of 1947 gives the director of the agency power to discharge employees without cause. It was the understanding of Congress at the time of CIA's enabling legislation that this unique power was needed to permit the removal of security risks summarily. A real catch-22 situation! Bill certainly was never considered a security risk, but that was the mandate that Admiral Turner used to conduct his reduction in force (RIF).

Mitch asked the agency for permission to sue them and they reviewed the case which took a long time. Turner left the agency, and Carter left the White House. The *Washington Post* wrote about us. Things seemed to move faster after these events occurred. The "Request to Sue the Agency" was passed from the CIA to the Civil Service Commission for their review. In August 1982, the Civil Service Agency advised us that: (1) Yes, there was age discrimination in the dismissals but, (2) the Director of CIA, by law, did have the indiscriminate right to hire and fire and therefore (3), the only resolution to the situation was to take the matter to court. We had won Round One! We had received permission to sue the agency! Bill did not really want to do this; all he wanted was his job back.

Mitch prepared to take the case to court but just as we were prepared to go to trial, a funny thing happened. Bill got a telephone call from the CIA. Would he like to come back to work? They needed him. Of course, this had nothing to do with his lawsuit. Mitch tried to get back pay, allowances, lawyers' fees, but to no avail. That would be admitting guilt on the part of the agency. Bill had said all along that all he wanted was his job back, and that was what was being offered. Nothing more and nothing less. Mitch generously refused to bill my husband for any of his services. The only charges were for his staff's services which was a considerable amount of money, but we thought it well worth it. It took three years and eight months before Bill returned to work in August 1982. He worked for another ten years, was promoted, and became eligible for retirement, which we are now fully enjoying. Sometimes principles can overcome personalities. We are both grateful.

Marry Me and You Are Fired

I met my husband, Larry, while we were both employed at the American Legation in Stockholm, Sweden, during the war. I'd had to flee from the Germans during the occupation of Norway (1940-1945). When the war ended, I had returned home to Oslo, and Larry was drafted into the United States Army. In due course, he was assigned to the War Department Detachment in Heidelberg, Germany. I later went to France as an "au pair" and we met regularly in Paris or in Strasbourg. We were young and in love!

We decided to get married, and in December 1947, I went back to Norway to prepare for the wedding. After Larry finished his military service, he took civilian employment, ostensibly with the Department of Army Detachment. When he arrived in Oslo for the wedding, he informed me that he had been fired because he was marrying a foreign national. He claimed that since his contract was being terminated, he had to be returned to the US at government expense. However, his executive officer claimed that Larry had voluntarily quit and, therefore, he had to get home at his own expense. This was all very confusing to me. Larry advised the office that he should be allowed to return to work in Germany because he was willing to work there. While on our honeymoon in Norway, Larry received a telegram stating that he was allowed to return to work in Germany, but that I was not allowed to join him. What a wonderful start to married life!

Larry was aware that there was a law permitting foreign nationals to gain US citizenship in thirty days, provided that the American citizen spouse was gainfully employed overseas. We decided that there was more than one way to make this happen. I would go to the

States and stay for thirty days with my uncle in Alabama while waiting for my citizenship papers to be processed.

Upon his return to Germany, Larry informed the executive officer of our plans and asked for contact instructions for me to use upon my arrival in the US Headquarters (although I did not know *which* headquarters at that time), in its infinite wisdom, stated that no provisions existed for a person to gain citizenship in thirty days. After numerous exchanges of cables, they finally had to concede that such a law did exist. My case paved the way for others to utilize this law and get their foreign spouses US citizenship without the required residence requirement.

In February 1948, when it was time for me to leave Norway, there were no passenger ships with space available going to the US from northern Europe. I finally found a Norwegian freighter that would take a few passengers, and so I set out for the unknown. The freighter took seventeen days, fourteen of them on stormy seas, to get from Norway to Philadelphia. I was, of course, seasick the entire voyage. In Philadelphia, the immigration authorities gave me a hard time, since I evidently did not have all the necessary papers. I had to stay on board the freighter overnight. I had visions of Ellis Island or returning to Norway on the same ship, this time with coal as company. However, the next day they let me go—I am still not quite sure why, but did not ask. I just went to Alabama to wait for my naturalization papers to be processed in Washington. After thirty days I left for Washington, and on my arrival, I used my contact instructions to arrange for the delivery of my passport. It took several weeks before I was able to get my American passport. My contact told me that I would be leaving for New York on a certain date to fly from there to Paris and then Larry would meet me. Later they informed me that this was changed and that I would be flying to Frankfurt, Germany. They told me they would inform Larry of this change of place and time—but they never did! Fortunately, I had learned fast how to deal with the bureaucracy and sent my own cable.

My passport and tickets were delivered to me at the railroad station in Washington a few minutes before the train departed for New York. Later, on board the airplane to Germany, I took a more careful look at the passport and in my military entry permit to Germany, it stated "Dependent of Lawrence, an employee of the Central Intelligence Agency." This was the first time I realized that Larry was a spy working for the CIA.

I was always very well received by Larry's coworkers and by all the other wives. We were stationed in Europe for many years, and then I went to Taipei, Taiwan while Larry was in Vietnam. Support there for "Saigon Wives," as we were so endearingly called, was minimal. I sometimes felt we worked for a different agency while our husbands were in Vietnam. It is not always just the "spy who is out in the cold." It can be cold out there for wives, too.

Chapter X

WOMEN AND CHILDREN FIRST

It won't happen to me. I came here for two years and I'm going to stay for two years. Wrong! We all remember the helicopter taking off from the top of the embassy in Saigon in April 1975. But there were other less-publicized departures in all parts of the world. Women and children fleeing on a moment's notice, leaving loved ones and possessions and favorite teddy bears behind. Armed guards and barbed wire, gunfire and angry crowds often escorted them away. They stood tall and made the most of difficult circumstances, long separations, and lonely days and nights.

Be Prepared for Eight Hours of Inconvenience

We were young and idealistic and it was our first tour overseas. I remember stopping in Hong Kong on our way to Vietnam, or South Vietnam as it was called in those days. We had finished our training at the farm and met our fellow "JOTs" (graduates of the intensive Junior Officer Training Program down on the "farm") at a cocktail party in Washington. They were also young and idealistic. One of them even pontificated about the wonders of Barry Goldwater all evening. Several of us stopped in Hong Kong on the way out, which was a passionate, romantic place. We took the Peak Tram up to the top of Victoria Peak and I stood there in the setting sun as it glistened on the Star Ferry and the billowing sails of the Chinese junks in the harbor. "Love Is a Many Splendored Thing" embraced me. I said to William Holden, aka my husband, "I would love to come back here and live some day."

"Perhaps," he said, "perhaps."

One of our fellow travelers had left Washington later than we did and had new information about our assignments in Vietnam. The CIA was sending us out to Vietnam by the dozens and shooting darts at a map to decide where we would go. We found out that our assignment was to be Danang. We got out our Esso road map and couldn't find it. Then one of the scholars among us discovered that it was still called Tourane on the old map. There it was—right up by the border with North Vietnam. Yes, this was going to be interesting!

We said farewell to the last bit of civilization I thought I would ever see and boarded an Air Vietnam Caravelle airplane for Saigon. There were many reporters on the flight as the Gulf of Tonkin incident had just occurred. I sat next to a young reporter who was conferring constantly with the stewardess (before it was politically correct to call them flight attendants) as to where we were and peering out the window as we flew over the Gulf. Kalb was his name and his brother was also on the flight. "How many ships do you see?" he asked. "Seven," I said, peering down. He wrote it down. That's the way the war was reported in those days. If you didn't get a story on an airplane, you got it in the rooftop bar of the Caravelle Hotel in Saigon.

The stench was overpowering as we landed at Tan Son Nhut airport in Saigon. We were met by some friends who were now experts, having been there for five full days. All had jeeps, and we piled our belongings in and went *in the heat of the night* to the Astor Hotel on Tu Do Street downtown in the "Pearl of the Orient." "Let's go out to dinner," they suggested. I stared at my husband which told him I did not want to go. There had been several incidents where grenades were tossed in restaurants frequented by foreigners. He calmly suggested that I was going to have to eat once in a while in the next two years and it might be a good time to start. I realized the insanity of my behavior and ran, not walked to the restaurant around the corner. It had metal grates all around it and barbed wire on top and we sat in the back of the place as we had been trained to do. It also had the best crepe suzettes I have ever eaten. I was terrified but I got over it. Shortly after the first BaMeBa, the local beer, I became a real expert on terrorism. Rumor had it that they cleaned out the bottles with formaldehyde and that was what produced the mammoth hangovers we had. Another reason could have been the number of bottles consumed. We made it through the dinner and I was able to return to the hotel at a slightly slower pace.

My husband called me the next morning from the embassy, but I did not know it. "You were in the shower. They told me at the desk." How did they know, I mused. I saw Viet Cong on every corner for two days. But I got over it fast. By the end of the first week, I'd taken a taxi to the Central Market to shop, traded dollars for piasters in elevators in hotels to get the best black market rate, eaten steaks on top of the Rex Hotel Officer's billet, and watched the Viet Cong hit bases outside Saigon while sipping brandy on a rooftop restaurant. So began my love affair with Asia that continues to this very day, some thirty-five years later. Love affairs are exciting, clandestine, passionate, deliciously happy, and tremendously sad. My life was to prove to be all of this.

A week after we blew into Saigon, my husband left for Danang. I had to wait for housing up there so I moved into the Saigon Palace apartments, also on Tu Do Street. I got a job as a contract wife at the station in Saigon until I could move north. Many of our friends lived in the same apartment building and we had a floating cocktail party most nights. Fighting the war from the trenches of luxury was difficult. Work hard, play harder. Stop by the Cosmos bar after work and mull over the events of the day. There was a coup every other week. We were ordered to stay in during these coups. Listen to Air Vietnam and they would tell us when we could come out. Some of our young, illustrious case officers wanted to be the first to report what was going on. So, after a few beers at the Saigon Palace, we would all pile into a jeep, beer in hand, and drive the streets looking for tanks and bad guys and a coup. The reporters might report from the rooftops but we went into the action. That was the first time I saw the "Zippo" monk. I lost it. He was in front of communications headquarters, standing there with his shaved head and saffron robe. Crowds were all around him, screaming in an unknown language. All of a sudden the monk sat down, doused himself in liquid and took out a Zippo lighter. Zip, zip, zip, burn. There was nothing left of him in ten minutes. I leaned over, threw up, and had another beer. It did not take long to get hardened to the tragedy of war.

The move to Danang took place about two months later. I got a job up there with the base, managing all the Vietnamese that worked for us. We found a house we liked next door to the "Blue Swallow" whorehouse and across the street from General Thi, the military officer in charge of the Northern Region of South Vietnam, fondly identified as I Corps. I often sat with my morning coffee as the American officers backed their jeeps out of the "Blue Swallow." I waved; they blushed. A man's gotta do what a man's gotta do.

It was a glorious life. How strange that sounds to me today. We had a Nuong guard in front of the house twenty-four hours a day. We ducked when rounding corners in our jeep because the Viet Cong had been throwing grenades into jeeps in Danang. We went to China Beach during siesta time each day with our weapons and a picnic lunch. This was long before the television show made the place famous. I learned to water ski on the Danang River. The US navy seals were frequently in town on R&R from their unbelievably difficult tasks in North Vietnam. Their heads would turn when they saw a Caucasian female in a bikini on water skis flowing up the river through the center of town. I liked the seals. They drank, they swore, they screwed, and they fought like hell for us in Vietnam. Oh yes, I was changing. The war even changed contract wives. I remember standing at the airport when our best friend was brought in from Quang Nam. One leg had been blown off in a skirmish with the Viet Cong. I learned to cry and then carry on. I had been there for seven months; the little girl was gone. I had gotten settled in and knew the ropes. Drank with the Aussies, worked with the Vietnamese, ate with the troops at the Doom Club at the airbase, drove a jeep with the best of them, and fired a weapon like a pro. I was ready for this tour.

Then the unthinkable—a radio broadcast on Air Vietnam and an announcement from President Lyndon B. Johnson. More incidents in the Gulf of Tonkin had caused the US to rethink its position and Johnson had ordered the bombing of North Vietnam and the evacuation of all dependents of US Government employees. The police action in Vietnam was about to become a war. Johnson was bringing in HAWK missiles, and we had to go. Surely that did not mean me! I had a job, no kids, experience, and pure unadulterated enthusiasm for this place and these people. The office could not get along without me. Why, they couldn't even call Saigon on the telephone. We heard the announcement and two hours later an MP from the US Army was knocking at our door. He handed me an official piece of paper that said "You are to be evacuated tomorrow morning, 9 February, 1965, on an Air Force plane. This evacuation is mandatory for all dependents . . .You should be prepared, therefore, for a period of inconvenience of approximately eight hours."

Where were we going? What do we take? Will we come back? That night was filled with tears, declarations of love, much laughter, so many friends, much scotch, it sends chills through me as I write.

The next morning we approached the airbase, where throngs of newsmen from all over the world were waiting. We were the first plane out, to be followed in the next two weeks with all dependents from Saigon. We had been warned by the station not to talk to the press. There were two of us from the base in Danang and four children. We joined the other government agencies' dependents and those who had been flown down from Hue. *Time Magazine* captured it for posterity. Lonely waifs with two small suitcases bidding farewell to husbands and not knowing where or when (we never thought "if") we would see them again. Shots were given in the hangar, passports had been flown up from Saigon on an Air America plane the night before. We were handed a box lunch from the Officers Club, kissed them all goodbye. Military and civilians had come to say goodbye, and thanks for bringing some semblance of sanity to our lives, if only briefly. The Vietnamese I worked with were outside the fence, crying and passing me gifts.

We boarded the C-130 aircraft that had been made available to carry us away. Jump seats lined the sides of the aircraft and we strapped ourselves in. Peering out of tiny windows as we soared over the HAWK missiles that were being unloaded to do their duty the next day. We flew over Marble Mountain, Monkey Mountain, China Beach, my house. Goodbye to a life I will never know again—and never forget.

It was a long trip with no announcements, no sounds except the roar of the engines as we peered out at the water below, seeking some clue to where we might be going. We stared off into space, too stunned to speak about the hours when our world was turned upside-down. And then we started to descend. It was dark, and we couldn't see a thing. Faint lights in the distance. Closer, closer. Oh, my God! Can it be? And there it was: the Fragrant Harbor and an island. A tiny beacon in the night; I saw the Star Ferry and the lights of Hong Kong.

I became a believer in the saying: "Don't Wish For something. You Might Get It." I spent the next two years working as a contract wife in Hong Kong. I lived in the apartment building where Han Su Yen wrote "Love Is a Many Splendored Thing." William Holden, aka my husband, stayed in Danang for his tour. He came to visit when he could. And my love affair with Asia continued.

Evacuations

I understood the fragility of our lives when one morning in June 1967, I got a frantic message from my husband, a case officer who was at his office in Tripoli, Libya, to quickly evacuate our cement-block white-washed villa with our two-year-old daughter and just-weaned Saluki puppies. He told me to bring what I could in a suitcase and drive to the base. The idea then germinated that no material possession would ever have such meaning to me that I could not lose it.

We had lived in Tripoli on a jagged dirt alley, with our toddler daughter, a wringer washing machine that sometimes worked, and a unique collection of antiquities. Still, we managed elaborate and clandestine entertaining. What would be called the Six Day War between the Arabs and Israelis had erupted. Retaliation by fire, looting, and bombing directed toward the imagined enemy ensued. Our villa was owned by a Jewish man, and so it was certain that all of our material possessions would be lost. Fortunately, I came to terms with it and a kind of peace carried me along. My daughter and I became refugees, and returned to Libya three months later.

Somalia Under Siege

The geographic direction of my life had been guided by an unseeing bureaucracy. We were assigned to Bangui, Central African Republic. We learned to savor the idea of living by the Ubangi River. Then the offer was abruptly canceled. Again and again, other posts were offered. Our hopes rose, only to be dashed by some bureaucratic snafu or wavering circumstances.

In January 1970, we finally moved to Mogadishu, Somalia. In the middle of winter in snowy Virginia where we had just purchased coats, leggings, mittens, boots, and skates, we headed to the equator where every day was guaranteed to provide a private sauna. After putting our house on the market twice during the erratic job offers, we now were forced to rent it. Our son and daughter were young enough to be caught up in the enthusiasm for adventure and ideas of seeing wild animals like Elsa from their favorite movie, *Born Free.*

We would have diplomatic cover, which meant we'd acquire the distinguishing titles. Our lives would become a daily challenge fraught with lingering stress and slashes of danger, but always with a rising excitement and wonder as to where this adventure would take us.

In this remote capital in East Africa, my husband, along with a telecommunications man, was replacing several case officers. The beleaguered group, along with foreign service people, had been declared *persona non grata* and they and their families had to leave the country in twenty-four hours. The "State Department diplomats" had been accused of espionage by the Somali government. Their children were yanked out of school and, after a hasty packing of bare necessities, they were on a plane out of there. Someone at the embassy supervised the packing of their household possessions, which would catch up with them three months later.

So it was essential that we play the diplomatic family role convincingly. My husband would be reporting back to Langley on affairs of the turbulent anti-American government of Somalia. For weeks before leaving the US, I was given private instructions on how to assist in basic "spycraft" such as retrieving "dead-drops," losing a "tail," and effective ways of protecting one's cover.

Nothing could have prepared me for the three months of persistent fear while living under a death threat. In 1972 the American ambassador to Sudan and his deputy chief of mission were killed in Khartoum, Sudan, at a reception. *Black September*, a terrorist group associated with the Palestinian Liberation Organization (PLO), took credit for the deed. The group managed to escape to Mogadishu, Somalia, and they were in our backyards. A written veiled threat against Americans was received at the embassy. Fingers of fear touched every area of our lives.

The embassy took immediate action to beef up security. Security measures on all levels were implemented, from the simple posting of buckets of broken glass on each stair landing of the embassy, in case of attack (these would be thrown on the steps to slow down the terrorists—shades of boiling oil being poured down from castle turrets), to beefing up the number of marine guards assigned to the embassy. All personnel and spouses were individually instructed on measures to take, like always changing routes and times when going about business, being alert to any subtle changes around me, and exercising caution and suspicion in every aspect of life.

Black September had not been accused of kidnapping or killing children, but why not? They were unpredictable. The CIA issued a small revolver to my husband to give to me to carry in my purse. My target practice had been cursory, but if pressed to the wall, I could perform. The Somali government did not want to take any action to expel the terrorists, as they were concerned with their relations with Arab countries. Nerves frayed under pressure.

The resident Americans' reactions were as diversified as Americans are. Secret knowledge of some Jewish ancestors nibbled at the edges of some people's anxieties. Others whose marital relations were not very strong, or whose personal coping skills weakened under such nightmarish stress, fled the country. Others took refuge in their homes, refusing any social engagements. There were those, too, who became sharper and stronger with each passing day, as if their entire life experiences, their faith, their trust in God would carry them through.

There was immediate fear for the life of the American ambassador's wife. Her family history went back to the powerful international House of Rothchild, the Jewish banking family. A false passport and disguise were created, and she was whisked away to safety. The *Black September* group stayed at their headquarters directly across the street from the American embassy in the PLO office, which was upstairs over a *meshawi* or grilled mutton-on-a-spit shop. Every time I entered the embassy I, like everyone else, had a feeling of being easy prey to a hail of machine gun fire.

Once, during a meeting in his office, the American ambassador, who happened to casually glance out of his window, yelled "Get down!" as he plunged to the floor, and everyone in the room crashed in unison like tin soldiers. He had spotted a figure with what appeared to be a machine gun in his hand on the roof across the street over the PLO office. It was another false alarm, but it underlined the tensions felt.

After three months of constant tension and diplomatic pressures exerted, the Somali government finally, very quietly, asked the *Black September* terrorists to leave, and they did. In a clarifying moment, as in a retraction of the predicted doom of a cancer, I understood the fragility of our lives.

Chapter XI

OUT IN THE COLD

This chapter is dedicated to the true "Silent Warriors." You know who you are. In memory of Eva G. who died this year. Our love, honor, and respect for a life well lived *under deep cover*.

Eulogy for Eva G.

Mama, can we talk about the Between Time?
I want to pick up the scattered pieces
of moments we shared.
After I came and
Before you left:
Memory shards so full of love they cut to the bone!

Mama, why are you crying?
What are the tears for?
You said: I weep for joy
Long you've been a hope, and
Now I hold you, precious one!

Mama, Mama! That pie you're making:
Can we make one, too?
You said: Kjariste, you and your sister
Will make a fine pie for Papa!
Roll it out and pat it with love
Now drop a kiss of jam into it
And in the oven it'll go!

Mama? Where are we going?
What are all the suitcases for?
You said: darling, we're leaving for America,
Sweden and Finland,
The Netherlands and Norway,
Thailand and Germany, too.
Watch your brother for me while I pack,
won't you?

Mama, let's talk about the Between Times
Of my coming and your going:
The days I played without a care

While you cared,
And cared,
And cared.
Let's talk about the nights
I hugged your perfumed pillow
Till sleep drew up blankets of comfort
all around me.

Mama, I remember your hands:
Blue-veined, shapely and strong
Smoothing a fevered brow
Teasing out snarls, as we howled
Folding our clothes, stirring sauce,
And pulling a needle loaded with silken floss
Through yards of Christmas cloth.

Mama, dearest Mama, I remember how
you snatched your rest:
Pouring over the paper, sipping coffee
And pondering puzzles;
Combing the shoreline for fossilized stones
And pretty shells;
Walking through woods: A root, weathered
and wizened,
Brought home as prized sculpture!

Mama, I remember a bad time too:
Deep currents of pain swept you away
To a land where you couldn't take us.
So we cared for the husk you left behind
Tearfully, tenderly, till twelve years passed.

Mama, darling, now it's me holding you
Do you know we're here?
Smoothing your fevered brow
As we care, and care, and care?
I remember the nights
holding vigil by your side
Pulling up a blanket to comfort you
While singing our heavy-hearted lullaby.

Mama, Mama, you can't be leaving!
Why can't you stay awhile?
You said with your eyes: Dear heart,
Even a Mama hasn't all the answers!
Just let me go. I suffer so.
Please let me go!

Mama, now it's me
Crying hot tears of joy!
You are free, precious one, free.
With a life well-lived, left behind
Kjariste Mola-mi!

Written by Britt Weaver
September 12, 1998

Confessions of a Deep Cover Wife

I met the man I would marry during the summer of 1950. He was enrolled as a GI Bill graduate at a summer school for American students at the university and lived in half of an outbuilding owned by a friend of mine. The other half of the building was a chicken coop; decent housing was as hard to come by as, well, fresh eggs. Jim didn't spend much time in class, but that was just fine with me. We were having a ball, taking dips in the icy waters of the fjord, getting sun-dried on the beach, climbing a small mountain to reach the secluded grassy knoll by the pool at its summit, jumping from stone to stone in the stream gurgling behind my parents' summer cabin. But as all good things must, our summer idyll came to an end, and we headed in separate directions—I to school in London and he to work in a third-world country. But before we parted, on a knoll above the hen house, in the cool light of the midnight sun, Jim said he'd like to spend more time, like a lifetime or so, with me. There was one little thing, however, that he thought he should tell me.

Jim had gotten his cover job in a radio station on his own. His boss in Washington had laid a Darwinian truth on him to the effect that if he could develop his own cover, fine; it would then be natural and durable. If he couldn't devise a credible occupation to conceal his connection with old Mother KUBARK, as the CIA was known to case officers in the early days, his boss told Jim that he could always be pulled back and stuck somewhere. In those days before the onset of bureaucratic sclerosis there was no psychological assessment, no committee review, no cover staff to set up a cover job. Just do it. Jump out into the waters of the real world, and sink or swim. Jim's handmade cover proved durable enough. It held up for sixteen years spent in five different countries and was strong enough to carry a family with four fine children, all of them born abroad. Jim joked that it cost too much to have babies in the States.

Looking back, I have to say that life under nonofficial cover, as it was called, had both advantages and disadvantages. I sometimes felt lonely as a nonofficial American denied access to official Americans in the diplomatic community, some of whom I knew from Langley but dared not acknowledge abroad, except in the settings of infrequent station parties where outside case officers and their wives could socialize with their inside colleagues. At one such party, the wife of an official cover case officer whose name has been banished from my memory talked to me about some work my husband was handling which I had no knowledge of. Her husband had told her about some amusing aspect of Jim's work. I was embarrassed by appearing stupid, but that was nothing compared with the deep hurt I experienced from realizing that Jim had not told me about an incident at work that a colleague of his had told *his* wife. When I confronted my husband, and suggested that he apparently didn't fully trust me, he only said that in honoring his secrecy agreement he was right and the colleague who talked "out of school" to his wife was wrong. End of episode, or so I thought. But this incident, that clouded our marriage by calling into question the indispensable bond of mutual trust, continued to bother me until Jim took early retirement at fifty.

To return to the happy flip side of being out in the nonofficial cold, it was a real privilege to be in a position to pick my own friends without reference to the diplomatic circle's nomenklatura, their silly cocktail parties, and their career-induced friendships.

In the same vein, I felt stimulated by the challenge of learning to live in a foreign environment, forced to learn a foreign language, and strange customs. I think that this made me a better, or at a least wiser, person and developed a healthy understanding and appreciation of foreign cultures in our children that made them better citizens of our shrinking world.

I sometimes missed American steaks and easy-to-cook frozen foods, available at the Post exchange and commissaries that were off limits to intelligence officers without any visible connection with the US government.

But I thoroughly enjoyed both the preparation and consumption of many of the indigenous foods that made up the diet of families under cover.

Speaking of food, I'd have to say that one of the big disappointments in our situation arose during one particular tour of duty that required Jim to be on the road at least half of the time. On TDY (temporary duty), he ate well, to put it mildly, in some of the finest restaurants in Europe. Some of his gourmet meals were paid for out of his per diem funds, but the tabs for the really sumptuous meals, accompanied by three different wines and topped off with a forty-year-old Napoleon Cognac, were written off as operational expenses. Once Jim wrote off his initiation fee and a year's membership at the Gaslight Club, a key club, in Paris. When the accounting item was questioned by a finance officer, who had seen some pretty outrageous expense claims in her time, Jim explained that joining the key club was the only way he could think of to ditch the tail he knew the opposition had put on him and his luncheon guest. *Security considerations* was used, nearly always successfully, to justify a variety of excesses in the good old days.

Not that I begrudged my husband his gourmet meals. It was just that while he was away, I had been forced to dine with the kids, enjoying such exciting entrees as hot dogs, macaroni and cheese, and rice pudding. Once on his return, I suggested that we might get a baby sitter and go out for dinner. The pained expression on his face said it all: He was filled with smoked salmon, goose liver pate, and filet mignon béarnaise. Enough of haute cuisine. All he wanted was some solid down-to-earth cooking. How about some hot dogs? That I didn't kill him on the spot will stand as a lasting tribute to a degree of self-control that went well beyond the known limits of human restraint.

Still, I wouldn't have traded my life as a deep cover wife for any other life I can imagine. Except for that bitch telling me about my husband's work.

Under Cover Child—Life Outside the Embassy

The daughters of the embassy officers had petticoats. I didn't because my father was under cover, which meant that we lived on the local economy. These girls had lots and lots of petticoats and they wore them all at once. And they had lunch boxes. With characters on them and cake inside. Not birthday cake, just plain old no-special-occasion cake with pink frosting. The kind of cake we never had. And cake that I couldn't have taken to school anyway, because it would have been mashed into a pulp in my plain old brown bag.

The official families could shop at commissaries full of low-cost goods that could be baked and wrapped in plastic—not wax paper—for lunches. They had PXs with little-girl clothes that belonged on princesses, and stints back in the States where their American moms would get up to speed on the latest stuff little girls should have. Like tights that were opaque, unpatterned. Not patterned brown woolens that attached to garters. Not quaint plaid smocks like all the little French girls wore to school. Why on earth would I want to look like a little French girl?

Somehow, not having these "things" never excluded me from the Dutch, the Finns, the Norwegian kids who lived in my "on the economy" neighborhood. Their parents shopped in the same stores Mom did. The corner butcher, the baker next door, the neighborhood dress shop. I wasn't aware of "things" at all when I played with them. Language was a barrier, but one that was soon overcome. Well, never quite in Finland, and my differentness, my specialness as an American, was occasionally resented, even by three-year-old Finnish children. Yes, cruelty starts very young, and particularly so in a society traumatized by a terrible war.

But my Dutch and Norwegian and Finnish pals and I didn't play with things usually. We played with our imaginations. We pretended to be Ivanhoe and Robin Hood. We rang doorbells and snuck into buildings. We romped through sewers and played tag and climbed on construction equipment and built tree forts and skipped rope. Our parents couldn't afford petticoats and cake every day. They saved a bottle of Coke for weeks, out on the third-floor gutter, where it tantalized my sister and me into climbing out at our peril to borrow a sip or two.

It was a wonderful time. So long as I wasn't in an American school, where my lack of the right accessories could make me feel more excluded than any foreign language ever did.

Chapter XII

THE NEXT GENERATION

They also served our country—they who rode school buses with armed guards and grates on the windows, were evacuated from cities under siege in the middle of the night, made friends and left them when their parents moved and had never, ever eaten a McDonald's hamburger by the time they were five years old. One daughter of a case officer told us of her experiences. Her father, a Russian speaker and Soviet expert, had been entertaining Soviets in his home for years. They had been assigned to Europe, South America, and Africa. She worried about all these strange people that kept visiting under cover of darkness. Finally, when she turned sixteen, he sat down and told her he actually worked for the Central Intelligence Agency and the KGB was his target. With a sigh of relief she exclaimed: "Thank God! For all these years I thought you were a Russian Spy!"

The Agency Brat

Until I was eighteen, I assumed that all children grew up the same as I, that they all experienced living in eight foreign cities during their adolescence . . . were the "new kids" in about twelve schools . . . traveled to at least a dozen different countries in their lifetime . . . and, more importantly, that everyone lived amongst different cultures and socio-economic conditions.

Then I came to America, which was about as foreign to me as a kid from Milwaukee moving to Djibouti. Yes, I had been back to the States on home leave but it wasn't "home" I was going to; "home" to me was and had been Bangkok or Manila or Hong Kong. So, the experiences I had of "going home" were never really going home but going to see my grandmother, whom I adored and miss deeply to this day. And, in fact, on home leaves, while good fun, there was always the anticipation of going back home to Bangkok or Manila or Hong Kong. "Living abroad" to me would have been living in America.

Leaving Hong Kong at eighteen, I entered a period of cultural shock and even a feeling of let down, disappointment. For America, interestingly enough, was always described to me as the Big Hope, the land of milk and honey, of opportunity. America to me was clean-paved streets, houses in neat rows where it was expected that everyone behaved in more or less the same way, a sanitized supermarket, a twenty-four-hour drug store, a place where everyone dressed the same, and cars, cars, cars.

America was not peddlers selling guava on the street; getting noodles at the "shack," which truly was a wall-less shack: it was not vibrant with the colors of red-and-gold glitter pasted onto building sides as a way of prayer; it was not using dried coconut shells to wax the floor; it was not an array of dress walking down the streets, from amah black pants/white top to beautiful sarongs mixed in with the standard suits; it was not bicycle peddlers and taxis mixed in with cars on the street or people gracefully carrying rice or vegetables with a stick across their shoulders and two baskets. Nor was it open markets where you didn't dare look too closely at the grime because the food you received was so delicious; and it wasn't the sounds of multiple dialects from several Chinese languages, to British English, Dutch, and "American English" all bantering together against the chaotic noise of the street.

American "life" was not filled with going out to dinner on Tuesday evening with a Chinese delegation and having sea urchin, tripe or jelly fish put on your plate; going out with the "embassy" crowd and having a luxurious four-hour Italian feast on a rooftop, going with your father to devour seasonal Shanghai crabs. If anything, the American way was having pizza one night and McDonald's the next.

Most saddening, America wasn't using the Star Ferry as a way to get from the Island to Kowloon. To this day, I think of how much I took the Star Ferry for granted: how many times during sunset I took it across Hong Kong harbor without even looking at the little junks and sampans fighting for water space against huge tankers and liners, but rather spent the ten-minute journey yakking with my girlfriends about the latest bit of stupidity going on in my school. It is why, to this day, when on a business trip to New York, I never miss the opportunity to take the Staten Island Ferry because it reminds me of Hong Kong and the Star Ferry.

America to me was boring. I distinctly remember saying to myself after I returned, "Is this all there is?" In retrospect, it probably has taken me until now, at forty, to digest this new life, to think of America as home.

Being an "agency brat" distinguished me for some reason; somehow it placed me above the typical army brat. In my mind, anyway. But it did much more than that. Army brats lived on American bases in as close a facsimile of American life as possible. I think that because of their seclusion from the culture they lived in, they didn't have the opportunity to learn from the cultures all around them. By being an agency brat, our families mixed in with the societies of the countries we lived in. Next door to me could be the president of a Hong Kong bank, or someone from the Netherlands. Their children became the kids I climbed Hong Kong's mountain with or skipped school with. So, in essence, being "agency" forced me to be tolerant and observant of other ways of life, to be fascinated and respectful of their heritage.

I think that my past has something to do with why, although I live in a "neat" little suburb and do the suburban thing, of all the cities in the US, I like New York and San Francisco best. It is in these cities that I find Americans most tolerant of many cultures living and breathing together, where a reference to someone's color as a way of distinguishing them is not whispered, and where America is at the pinnacle of what it should be, a harbor for many nations. I was shocked that, as multi-cultural as America in theory should be, in fact, between the two coasts, the many faces of the world do not exist. It is why, as an adult, I chose to live near Washington, DC and not Montana or somewhere in the "middle"—because I simply could not allow my children to grow up intolerant of diversity.

I was stunned that the land of opportunity that opened its arms to the world, in fact, remains intolerant of cultural differences. I was deeply saddened that many immigrants coming to America, instead of being proud of their heritage, homogenized and, in many instances, elected to forget about their roots.

I am most thankful that by being an agency brat, I was able to live in Asia for most of my childhood, because I am half Chinese. I remember coming on "home leave" once and visiting a cousin who was just slightly younger than I and struggling to rid herself of being half Chinese and was embarrassed and embittered that she looked Asian. I am so proud of my heritage. In fact, it is why I chose to keep my maiden name. I am not so certain that, if I had grown up in America, given the intolerance I have found that exist here, I would be quite as proud of my heritage as I am today.

Because of this pride, my daughters, who are but one quarter Chinese, are very proud to be Chinese and tell people so. I am happy that their experience in America has made them proud to be both American and Chinese.

Now I am grown and have adjusted to living in America, but I have also done many things that allow me to continue to learn from different cultures. I sought out a company that would allow me to travel around the world thereby, expanding the vision I have of the world. I dream that someday I will be able to give my children the richness that my parents gave to me. I am doubtful that this will happen, but when my children are old enough to remember the smells, the nuances, and the faces of a country, I plan to take them to many places in the world. I want them to grow to be as rich as I am; rich because they have in their souls the sight of many faces.

I have come to believe, perhaps because of my experiences with moving to new locations and being the new kid in town, that "home" is not America, and it is not Hong Kong or Thailand either; it truly is where my children, husband, and parents live. Which, at the moment, is in a suburb in America.

Laos Showers

When I was eleven, we moved to Vientiane, Laos. I will never forget the day we got there. The moment the plane doors opened, the hot, sticky, moist air flew through the cabin in an instant, drenching us all with the realization that we had just arrived in a strange, new place.

We did not live in government housing. My mother wanted us to live in a regular house, off the American base, exposed to the people and the culture in a new place. I bless her for that now because I don't think I or my sisters would have had the experiences we did if we'd been isolated on base.

Our first house in Laos was huge and gray, covered with ivy and up high on stilts. It was the rainy season; after a few days we understood the necessity for stilts when we saw the roads and gardens covered with water and saw the water rise almost to the floor of our house. But it wasn't just the flooding that made my mother scream for a house change.

After we arrived and started moving in, I went upstairs to the bathroom to take a shower. The shower was in the middle of this huge bathroom, a stand-alone shower with a round shower curtain you pulled around yourself. The curtain hung from a round iron curtain rod. To start the shower, there was a metal ring to pull from the ceiling and the water from the shower head would rain straight down on you. The whole shower was up on a sloped platform so that the water would not only go down the drain at your feet, but would also pour down over the platform to a larger drain in the floor a few feet away. A curious set-up, I thought, as I got ready and pulled the curtain around me.

I yanked on the metal ring and the warm water

showered down, drenching me instantly. I suddenly felt something moving under my feet. I looked down and saw that out of the drain were crawling hundreds—literally hundreds—of huge, black, shiny cockroaches. They poured out of the drain in a black mass of squirming bodies. I know I must have leapt at least three feet in the air and I can swear to you that, as I flew screaming from the bathroom, my feet never once touched the floor. As I hollered for my mom as loud as I could, I kept dancing frantically around, checking my feet to make sure no monstrous black thing was crawling on me.

Finally, my mom came and I made her look in the bathroom. When she came out, she was puzzled. There was nothing there. No big monstrous cockroaches, no squirming, hideous bodies. Just water and a running shower. And that's when I *knew*. The whole bathroom setup was not to make sure the water went down into the big drain, but for the cockroaches! They would crawl from the small drain because of the shower water and get washed into the bigger drain on the floor. Afterward, they would crawl back up into the drain pipes until the next person to take a shower would start the horror show all over again. Aghast, I could not believe we were going to have to live in this house. Or, for that matter, in this country!

I insisted to my mom that we were going to have to move. She was not sure if my over-active imagination was running on high, so we waited and ran a test shower. Sure enough, the same thing happened. The sight was frightful to behold. Watching the huge, black, squirming bugs was enough to make the most hard-core horror fan feel faint and squeamish.

After we discovered that the house was swarming with cockroaches due to the flooding and the location, there was no way we were staying. We moved soon after. And, although my introduction to Laos was certainly a heart-stopping one, I went on to enjoy our tour and learned a great deal in the time we were stationed there.

Lucky Thirteen

It was the perfect summer. The recipe: A stock of wonderful weather, a smidgen of pepper, a pinch of adolescent kisses, a dash of excitement garnished with the bittersweet fruit of my first true love.

I know that there is a strong tendency when looking back in life to romanticize and idealize how things were, conveniently forgetting the bad and the ugly. In my case, I remember the summer of '72 with startling clarity, and the negatives simply aren't there. Nevertheless, my efforts to recapture the full beauty and splendor, the rapture of those three months, always seem to fall short.

We were in Frankfurt, West Germany, courtesy of my dad's work, which I first learned five years later was with the CIA, in an office in an old building. A US dollar bought about 3.5 Deutsch marks then, and my allowance of two dollars went a long way at the kiosk down the street, where big Gummi Bear candies sold for only five or ten pfennig apiece. I got an early taste of age discrimination, however, when I learned that the Army base movie house charged adults thirteen and over thirty-five cents, a whole dime more than the kids paid.

In this wondrous summer, even two terrorist bomb threats at the 3rd Armor Division where I went to school just meant that we got out early on both occasions. The Baader-Meinhoff loonies hadn't killed anyone yet, but later they did succeed in killing a major with a bomb that blew out the windows on the back of Dad's office building.

The weather at the foothills of the Taunus mountains could not have been better—just enough drizzle to water down the basepaths on the baseball diamond but not enough to cause a single game to be canceled. All in all a perfect setting for a field of dreams to come true. Yes, baseball was that summer's heart, body and soul, if not my entire raison d'être. The game provided a clock and needed discipline to the days and weeks, ensuring that not one minute would be squandered on idle pursuits. I've never before or since experienced as much nervous tension as I did when I tried out for the Frankfurt Babe Ruth league (thirteen to fifteen year olds). Having to field hard grounders at third, making accurate throws a mile across the field to first, taking ten swings at pitches thrown by an adult, with Dad the only supportive face in a crowd of a hundred strangers, knowing I was being judged and fearing no one would pick me to play . . . Wow, that was pressure that both elevated my adrenaline and nearly paralyzed me, and erased from my memory the details of how I had performed. I only recall that I had played well enough to be chosen for the team coached by Mr. Horan. That was quite an honor, because his teams always competed for the title. I started at third and had a good season, but more importantly, the team won the league championship. It was a great time for the boys of summer (Eddie, John, Pat, and the Marks brothers.)

For rare rainy days, my friend and I invented a great indoor game: a teenage adaptation of Monopoly. Our house, designated for housing a family of bird colonel rank, had a full basement. Half of it was used for laundry and storage; the other half was a spider-infested recreation room my older sisters were allowed to use. For months, Britt and Tina paid me to vacuum out the spiders. One day, I decided to see what would happen if I stopped messing with the Daddy Long Legs. It worked! The girls abandoned the place, leaving behind a stereo, two psychedelic lamps, a few black light posters, a card table and two old sofas. Everything that was needed for our game.

First, we had to find some girls who lived in the midrise NCO apartment houses and would be suitably impressed at being invited into officer's quarters. Two, sneak them past mom and, if caught going downstairs, cover the enterprise with innocence by asking for some lemonade and cookies for the game. Three, set up the board to make it look like the game had been going on for a while. Four, turn on the weird lights and some groovy music. Five—game time—start necking.

We were protected from discovery by the cellar stairs, which gave off a dungeon-like clanking sound, which allowed time to button up, turn on the ceiling lights, and take our places at the table, ready to roll the dice. We never considered that our unkempt appearances, flush faces, and heavy breathing would give us away.

All that play gave us huge appetites, so off to the orchards we'd go. The trees were laden with apples, peaches, plums, and pears, all ours for the taking. We seldom brought the girls on these forays, because we'd heard about the farmer who patrolled this garden of plenty with a gun loaded with rock salt. We didn't know what that was, but we figured it might be painful to find out. So, we devised a getaway plan—the Strassenbahn (trolley). There was a "strasse" stop a few hundred yards away, and at the first sight of any adult (not knowing what an armed peasant might look like), we dashed off to catch our chariot to freedom. A great idea, but paying for boarding the trolley would consume our meager allowances and leave no funds for staples at the kiosk. Our solution to the problem was creative, illegal, and fairly dangerous (in a word, stimulating)—ride on the tail end bumper of the trolley. Timing was of the essence: climb on too early and the driver would spot the action and call for the polizei; too late and the trolley would be moving too fast to hop aboard.

Then one day, everything changed. Her name was Ginger. She was the coach's daughter, the loveliest, sweetest girl I had ever met. This aspect of that summer I have trouble recalling clearly, for I was living a dream. I remember us talking, but none of the words. I remember the physical shock when our hands met, and our first kiss, but the rest of that day is a blank. I'll forever treasure the weeks we had together—they were magical—but they were only weeks, as our families were rotated stateside, hers to Camp Campbell, Kentucky, and mine to a DC suburb in Northern Virginia. We exchanged a few letters, but each of us moved on. As a service brat I guess you had to develop the ability to let go, or go crazy.

Perhaps the abrupt ending to my relationship with Ginger and my teammates served as punctuation to bracket in my mind's eye, a very special place and time.

I was thirteen, wore thirteen on my uniform and thirteen has been my lucky number ever since.

Wishful Fishing

My dad taught me how to fish. I still look forward to wetting a line and hooking the big one that dad assures me was, and still will be, out there—someplace.

We fished in many and varied places. On homeleave, it was off the end of the dock at Gull Lake near Kalamazoo, Michigan, where sunfish and bluegills literally couldn't wait to get at our bait at sundown. We marveled at the shimmering waters illuminated by that silvery cool midsummer midnight sun on the coast of the Gulf of Finland. Tasty siikaa (white fish) patrolled among the rocks and reeds near our harborside flat in Helsinki. The gurgling waters of a brook rushed down from the Skarven mountain in Valdres, Norway, where its mossy rocks provided totally secure hiding places for speckled trout. Lazy carp rested in the dark, still waters in the tiny feeder canal behind our house in Voorburg, Netherlands. And we fished in the eddying waters at the base of a small dam in the Taunus mountains just outside our housing compound in Frankfurt, where dad confessed he had unsportingly fished with hand grenades at the close of the war, (i.e., *his* war, WWII).

When fishing with my dad, I learned to distinguish between fish as a noun and an infinitive (pardon the pun)—i.e., to attempt to catch fish. I learned early on that a verb does not necessarily net a noun. This distinction persists despite the application of many strict fishing rules, to wit:

- The Time of Day Rule, requiring a 4:00 A.M. wake up to lure to the hook whole schools of drowsy fish eagerly looking to get the early worm;
- The Silence is Golden Rule, designed to keep secret from the fish your presence at the end of the

line, bottling up the natural itch for conversation like a volatile gas in a sealed bottle;

- The Tasty Tidbit Rule, whereby progressively larger amounts of freshly dug earthworms (bought worms totally unacceptable) are loaded onto hooks of various sizes, to hook shortsighted fish;
- The Rule of Perpetual Motion, in which the ever mobile quarry has to be pursued wherever they might be feeding: in that cove just ahead, or maybe back there.

I will say this for dad: His techniques charmed the children fish right onto our hooks. The sweetest little fishes swam away from their two-pound mothers onto our waiting snares, only to be released after we proudly showed them to Mom as evidence that fishing was not a time-wasteful pursuit. Far from it.

Fishing with my dad taught me that much of the fun in life comes in the anticipation and preparation for an activity; that patience alone does not guarantee success, but it may open doors to special moments nonetheless; that there's no shame in failing to achieve a goal; and that it's a doggone shame that some people stay in bed, asleep, when they could be fishing.

My Dad

People who knew my dad would understand that he never did anything like a normal person. One day he called us into our family room and he passed us a letter. The letter was in reference to his recent promotion to SIS-2 (Senior Intelligence Service). My first instinct, being sixteen years of age, was "Cool dad. Now that you got a raise, can I get a new car?" I failed to notice the logo on the top of the letter. My sister kindly pointed out that it said CIA. My reaction to where my dad worked was "Great, join the rest of the neighborhood." My parents had picked a perfect place to live as the majority of our neighbors worked for the Central Intelligence Agency.

My father told us he had not given us the true location or nature of his job in the past because he felt it was too difficult for children to keep their mouths shut. He was probably correct. We still couldn't keep them shut but he was now going overt and it did not matter.

Today, I wish I knew what my father did for the CIA for thirty-two years. He passed away two months after he officially retired in 1995. The agency absorbed all my father's life when I was young and spending time with him was very difficult. My brother and sisters and I feared him. He was never our friend like mom was. He was the man who came home late in the evenings and sat in his chair and read a book or watched TV and said very little or yelled. I now realize he was frustrated from his job at the agency and he couldn't vent his frustrations with my mom or us. I would meet people that worked with him and they would say "Your father is a wonderful man; he is so great to work for." I would just say, "Come home with me one evening and you may change your opinion."

I was young when my parents returned to the U S from their last tour abroad. My brother was diagnosed with dyslexia, so my father told the agency that he would not be able to go overseas again. My mother told me that this decision truly affected his career.

I was in college the last year my father was active at the agency. I attended a local university and lived at home. My classes were usually scheduled in the morning, and I came home in time for lunch. My dad never came home for lunch when I was young, but toward the end of his career he started to come home on a regular basis. I started seeing a sensitive side of him. One of the ladies who worked with my dad told me after he passed away, that as dad was leaving for lunch he would say "I am going home to have lunch with my puppy, Duncan," and she would say "No, you are going home to have lunch with your daughter." My father turned to her and said: "You know, Carol, I missed watching all my kids grow up because of the agency and now I am not going to miss this time with my daughter". Even after three years, I still cry when I tell this story.

My father's job affected me as an adult. I feel sad that I missed all that time with him. My most precious memories of my father are only the final years of his life, and that hurts me. I guess I should be grateful because I know there are kids out there who had abusive dads and I did not experience that. I just wish my siblings could have shared the time that I did with him—maybe they would understand why his passing affected me so much. It was like being given something that you have always wanted and then having it ripped away. If my father had been an accountant or a doctor he would have been able to come home from work and tell us about his horrible day, then be able to enjoy his evening with his family instead of sitting in a chair like an expanded balloon getting ready to explode. Maybe he passed away because he couldn't wind down from the life he lived for thirty-two years. Maybe it was something else. All I know is the agency got the best thirty-two years of my father's life.

Lies and Truths

Life as an agency dependent was very normal to me until I was eighteen, when I was finally told that I was an agency kid. During my years of development, I experienced several different reasons why I never had to question my father's authority. First of all, my father was certainly a man we never questioned twice, because he'd correct our need to be inquisitive the first time through his not-so-subtle and definitely not-so-quiet "discussions" with us. As teenagers, I think we challenged dad more than some of his colleagues and foreign adversaries with our new-found philosophies of life. Dad was quick to set us straight and we never dared to stray from his intended path for us. Dad's intentions for all four of us to take on a career in the business arena came true for three of us, and the fourth gave it his best shot until he finally got parental approval to veer off in a different direction.

Dad was and still is the smartest individual I have ever known. Not because he was my father and trained me to think this way, but because he knew everything. We loved to challenge his mental encyclopedia as much as possible. It was our life's goal to stump him one day. Anytime I could force my family into spending a little "quality time," QT as it was affectionately known in our house, it had to be in a way that would at least amuse my father into participating. Usually we selected "Trivial Pursuit" because it gave us a peaceful way of challenging our father's intelligence. After the second or third time of playing with him, it became pretty obvious that if Dad won the first roll the game was over. He'd answer every question correctly and would keep playing until all the wedges were accumulated. So, to doubt his way of thinking seemed absurd to us.

The truth came out about his career during the early summer of 1990. All the planets must have been aligned for this major revelation to come forth to his kids. My father's identity as a CIA employee was very covert, even to some of the people at the agency. My parents gathered all four of us together to show us a letter sent to my father. We were pretty oblivious to what was really going on because we had just finished another year of schooling and were mentally drained. My father made sure all four of us were sitting together on the sofa when he handed us the letter congratulating him on his promotion to Senior Intelligence Service (SIS) grade. Of course, not understanding government personnel rankings, this SIS status meant nothing to us except we understood our father had received a promotion. Hurrah! Yet another reason not to doubt his intelligence. Then my mother, with her keen sense in figuring out that we didn't get it, told us to look at the letterhead on the stationery. There at the top was the gold-embossed eagle's head emblem of the "Central Intelligence Agency." My first thought was that they put the letter on the wrong stationery. But my mother proudly confirmed that they had hidden this secret from us for our entire lives. Normally, the thought that your parent has a different job than originally told to you would not be a big deal. But I was now facing the fact that my father was a spy. This is not an easy concept to grasp and then move on in a few minutes. I don't think I was able to get out any of the questions I had racing through my head for about thirty minutes. I just looked at my father with shock and amazement. My mother explained that the truth was kept from us so we would not have to lie to our friends or teachers about what our parents did for a living. The only concept of espionage we had was influenced by the *James Bond* films. My father was quick to point out that the true life of a spy was nothing like that in a film. Of course, this was apparent, since my father was no suave, debonair, sharp dresser, or lady killer like Agent 007.

Nonchalantly throughout our talk, my parents

pointed out that our family friends were also in the same line of work. This list of individuals included every friend of the family we had ever seen on a regular basis. Whoa! You mean to tell me that not only were my parents' lying (remember, they called it "protecting") to me all these years, but so were the family friends I considered extended family? I was now seeing my entire life as a cover-up. Finally, after several hours of discussion, my parents reiterated that my father was still very much undercover and that we could not let the secret out.

My siblings and I were in complete shock the remainder of the week. To us, it was like he was a super hero out of a comic book. Clark Kent becoming Superman was less a miraculous feat than our father becoming super spy. You see, we never had a reason to doubt his word because it had always proven to be life's law, but now we had major grounds to question his word. After all, he had kept this information from us for almost twenty years.

Some signs were pretty apparent in hindsight. His fascination with reading novels on espionage history, the mysterious calls to go to work in the middle of the night, the trips he took when we did not know where he was going, the multitude of foreign families that he helped to establish in the Washington, DC, area, the foreign officials my parents would entertain when they were in town for business, and most obvious later on, the agreement to drop me off at my job near Langley, because it was convenient for him. My father rarely went out of his way for anyone, including his children.

Shortly after the shock wore off, my father allowed us to attend our first CIA Family Day. After a life-long cover-up, we kids were not going to miss this one—our first glimpse into the life my father had lived for almost thirty years. Driving through the guard gate at the main compound at Langley, Virginia was a complete thrill. I was absorbing as much as I could because I knew there was zero probability I would be allowed back. We proudly followed my father through the compound he knew so well—the impressive seal, etched into the floor in the main entrance, the hall of portraits of past agency directors, and the super-cool maze hallways. My father explained it was to prevent any chance of communication from being intercepted by satellite or radio receivers. Then he allowed us into his office area. My mind was racing with images of a super high-tech facility with all the gadgets any super spy would need. This was, of course, far from the truth when we walked through the combination-locked door to a very ordinary office. He showed us his office, which seemed pretty humble for a man of his rank. We were happy to see that he had our pictures on his desk. Of course, in his loving and affectionate humor, he said he had just put them out for that day and they would return to his drawer after we left.

In the years that followed, we came to the realization that our parents really were protecting us from lying. Keeping the information from our closest friends was difficult, but we kept our promise. We were fortunate to have a close circle of family friends and their kids (who had known about their parents and mine for several years but never divulged the news to us) to share and inquire about the lifestyle they had led. Similar to the Mafia, the CIA has a twisted way of keeping it's own "kind" together. All my family's associates were former spies or current spies. Whether it was picnics, cookouts, holiday celebrations, or weddings, the CIA "family" always seemed to be together. When my father passed away, they were the people we called first, even before our real family members.

During my father's life, he strongly encouraged us not to pursue a career with the agency, due to what he called "increasing bureaucratic bullshit." His influence allowed us to expand our tight-knit circle of friends with some in a more mainstream line of work. New friends I've made are fascinated with the international intrigue associated with my father's line of work. However, I let them know that life with a spy was as normal as theirs, except that their fathers planned corporate business strategies while mine planned embassy break-ins, assisted defectors and their families seeking asylum, and created counterintelligence strategies. Pretty normal life as I saw it.

CONTRIBUTORS

The authors wish to thank the contributors listed below and the many other women whose stories are included but who wished to remain anonymous.

KITTY ALBERT is a semi-retired news junkie who lives in Maryland, after many years overseas. Interests include cooking, golf, dogs and the Washington Redskins. She is currently involved in research study regarding the mystique of young Asian women in relationships with older American men.

DONNA S. BALCOM is a Michigan State University Graduate. She lived in Saigon as a CIA wife from July 1964 to February 1965, was evacuated, divorced, and is the mother of two children. She has been a teacher at Washington Business School since 1991. She was a teacher and director of education at Washington School for Secretaries from 1972 to 1991. She lives in Fairfax, Virginia.

PEG BEARDEN is a former agency employee, spouse, and mother of three grown sons. She spent seventeen out of twenty-one years of married life moving her family throughout Europe and Asia. She resides in Houston, Texas, working as a consultant for American Express Corporate Services.

LEILA WINSTEAD BROOKS is a former dancer at The Balcony, Bangkok. She cooks the best Mexican food this side of the Chao Phraya River and is a recently retired film editor and producer. Affiliations include DAR, CIRA, Colonial Dames of XVII Century, and Daughters of the Republic of Texas. She is an orchid grower, master gardener, and Republican. She is married to a former case officer and resides in Houston, Texas.

ANGELA GIRALDI was born in Newcastle upon Tyne. She worked for the British Foreign and Commonwealth Office in the late seventies and was posted to the British Embassy in Rome, where she met her husband, Phil. They served in various European and Middle Eastern posts before settling in Virginia. She is interested in quilting, gardening, and watercolor painting.

AUSTIN JAY GOODRICH resides in Grand Rapids, MI, where he's busy perfecting his role as Mr. Mom while rehabbing from an auto accident. Occasionally, he finds time to write, using his extensive travel and black sheep history to frame his stories.

TINA GOODRICH is married and the mother of two daughters. Tina is currently the executive director of the Industrial Designers Society of America. She graduated summa cum laude from the University of Wisconsin and has since discovered the pleasure of never ever moving!

ANNE JACKSON was born in Oslo, Norway. Her father, who worked for the Norwegian resistance after the Nazis occupied Norway in April 1940, had to flee to Sweden in the summer of 1943. Anne followed that autumn and met her future husband there. They have been married for fifty years and have two daughters, two grandsons, and one granddaughter.

SHERRY CANNISTRARO JAHODA, with her wonderful new husband, Joe, and two Himalayan cats, lives a tranquil life in Reston, Virginia. Her adventures, however, have continued with their involvement in archaeological explorations in Egypt on the Gizeh Plateau. Living in the states around family and friends with no ties to the CIA has brought a splendid balance and stability that would not have been possible earlier.

NAN MILLER is currently active in community volunteering, downhill and cross-country skiing, hiking, golfing and camping. She has been married over fifty years to a former training officer and lives in Sisters, Oregon.

JUDITH SAUNDERS O'REILLY is the mother of four children and a multitude of West Highland terriers and lives in Vienna, Virginia. Her motto: "Shut up, smile, and wear a low-cut dress". Married thirty-one years to the late John Patrick O'Reilly. If you can hear us John, we hope you've opened up an Irish Pub in Heaven to replace O'Tooles.

KELLY O'REILLY is the daughter of a thirty-two year career CIA officer. Kelly was born and raised in the Washington, DC, metro area. She received her BBA from Longwood College and her MBA from Marymount University. Kelly currently works in the telecommunications industry as a Financial Analyst and resides in Falls Church, Virginia.

MEGHAN O'REILLY was born in Manila, Philippines. Her father worked for the agency for over thirty years. She attended Marymount University in Arlington, Virginia and graduated with a degree in Marketing. She currently works for a marketing firm in Reston, Virginia. She resides in Vienna, Virginia.

LEIGH PLATT ROGERS was born in Camp Lejeune, NC and raised all over the world by virtue of her father's occupation and as a result, lived in Europe and Asia. She is a graduate of the College of William and Mary and currently resides in California with her husband. She is a Workers' Compensation Specialist for the Department of Transportation, Maritime Administration.

NANCY ROSS, after thirty years of marriage to a "kooky spook" and tours on three continents, is certain that her spot in heaven is secure. Her recipe for a successful life as a spy's wife is to take the job semi-seriously, the husband with a grain of salt, and life overseas with a walloping sense of humor. To keep sane, she teaches middle school, entertaining her students with vignettes from her past lives.

BRITT WEAVER works as a Learning Disabilities Resource teacher in the Fairfax County public school system. In her spare time she writes articles and pursues the craft further through classes and as a member of a writers' group. Discovering the sacred and the absurd in her life gives her plenty of material to write about. She is married and has two college-age daughters.

KATHLEEN WELLS is currently working for a major communications company in the Washington area. She divides her time between Northern Virginia and the Outer Banks of North Carolina. She shares her life with "someone special," two grown children and a grandson.

GLOSSARY OF TERMS

AGENT · Individual who is aware he is engaging in clandestine operations on behalf of a sponsor and submits to some degree of control by the clandestine organization

ASSESSMENT · The analysis of the motivations and qualifications of an agent candidate to determine his suitability for, and his susceptibility to, recruitment

BRUSH PASSES · A predetermined brief clandestine contact for passage of material, information or equipment

CASE OFFICER · Also referred to as an operations officer; one who recruits and/or handles agents as a staff member of an intelligence organization

COMPARTMENTATION · Procedures and practices designed to ensure that each member of a clandestine organization knows only what he need to know about the personnel, structure, and activities of the rest of the organization

COVER STORY · Devised story to conceal actual intelligence activities

CT PROGRAM · Career Trainee Operational Training Program for New Case Officers

DEA · Drug Enforcement Administration

DEAD DROPS · A concealed site established for transfer or passage of clandestine material, information or equipment

DI · Directorate of Intelligence (Analysis and Evaluation)

DO · Directorate of Operations

THE "FARM" · Internal slang for CIA training facility rear Williamsburg, Virginia

JOT PROGRAM · Junior Officer Training Program - Predecessor to the CT program

KGB · Committee of State Security (Soviet equivalent of FBI and CIA combined)

PCS · Permanent Change of Station - Assignments abroad for a specified period of time, normally two or three years

SAFEHOUSE · Facility used for clandestine operations

SURVEILLANCE · The observation of human or physical targets by human or technical means in order to acquire information concerning identities, activities and contacts of such targets

TDY · Temporary duty (term applied to individuals on short term temporary assignments)

TARGET · Person, thing, place, or action against which a clandestine operation is directed

TRADECRAFT · The methods and techniques unique to the conduct of clandestine activities

ABOUT THE AUTHORS

KAREN L. CHIAO was raised in the Midwest and had wanderlust from the age of five. She read as many books as possible about the world. She once tried to dig to China but to no avail. So she went there. Married forty years, she has one wonderful daughter and two adorable granddaughters. She met many wonderful people during her years with the CIA and counts most of them as cherished and dear friends. She will always be grateful for the opportunity to travel and live in so many foreign countries.

MARIELLEN B. O'BRIEN is of Russian heritage and was raised in a small town in Connecticut. Her lust for travel began with an elementary school field trip to New York City and a Girl Scout Jamboree in Pontiac, Michigan. She has traveled and worked with CIA in Washington, Austria, Vietnam, Hong Kong, Thailand, Denmark, and Los Angeles for over three decades. When not at an airport, she spends her time writing and lives on the Outer Banks of North Carolina with her husband.

ABOUT THE EDITOR

AUSTIN GOODRICH was first a writer, then a spy before retiring from the CIA to return to freelance writing. He is a published author. He spends his days trying to control his word processor. Good friend and great motivator for the two "old broads."

Philip Kent Master Photographer & Associates